Reese Ryan writes sexy, deeply emotional romances full of family drama, surprising secrets and unexpected twists.

Born and raised in the Midwest, Reese has deep Tennessee roots. Every summer, she endured long, hot car trips to family reunions in Memphis via a tiny clown car loaded with cousins.

Connect with Reese at ReeseRyanWrites on Instagram, Twitter and Facebook or at reeseryan.com/desirereaders.

The Billionaire's Legacy

REESE RYAN

MILLS & BOON

First published in Great Britain 2018
by Mills & Boon, an imprint of HarperCollins*Publishers*
1 London Bridge Street, London, SE1 9GF

Large Print edition 2018

© 2018 Roxanne Ravenel

ISBN: 978-0-263-08317-0

MIX
Paper from
responsible sources
FSC™ C007454

This book is produced from independently certified
FSC™ paper to ensure responsible forest management.
For more information visit www.harpercollins.co.uk/green.

Printed and bound in Great Britain
by CPI Group (UK) Ltd, Croydon, CR0 4YY

To my best friend, entrepreneur, aesthetician, makeup artist, proprietor of The Brow Snob, a cancer survivor and an all-around badass Tonie Jones. I'm thankful you just celebrated another cancerversary, and that we're still friends three states, two marriages, four children, two grandchildren and thirty-five years later.

To the amazing readers who faithfully read my books, fall in love with my characters and share your enthusiasm for my work with your friends and family online and off... I'm so grateful to have you as a reader. I honestly can't thank you enough.

Prologue

"Benji? Oh, my God, is that you?"

Benjamin Bennett shifted his attention to the source of the husky female voice he knew as well as his own.

"Sloane." He hadn't seen Sloane Sutton in nearly a decade yet he recognized her instantly. The passing years had been good to her; she was even more beautiful than he remembered. "I wasn't sure you were coming to the wedding."

Sloane wrapped him in a hug that seared his skin and sent electricity skittering down his spine. He released her reluctantly.

"I just decided a couple of days ago." Sloane smoothed down the skirt of her brilliant blue, floor-length gown. It hugged her heart-stopping curves, showing off the glowing brown skin of one toned shoulder. "I didn't even tell Delia I was coming."

That explained why his sister hadn't mentioned it.

"Well, it's good to see you, Sloane. You look... incredible," he stammered, his face and neck warm. The passage of time hadn't lessened Sloane's effect on him. He was as tongue-tied in her presence now as he'd been at fifteen.

His crush on her began the moment he'd first laid eyes on her. He was five years old and Sloane was ten.

"Thanks." Sloane beamed. "You look pretty darned handsome yourself."

"Blake must've been glad to see you." Benji nodded toward the groom. He loosened the collar of his shirt, which suddenly seemed too tight.

"It's good to see Blake so happy." Sloane's gaze softened, but sadness suddenly crept into her voice and clouded her brown eyes. "Savannah seems really sweet, and their baby, Davis, is adorable."

"He's a cute kid," Benji acknowledged, shoving

his hands in his pockets and shifting his weight to his other foot. "And Savannah is really sweet. You'll like her."

Getting to the altar hadn't been easy for his cousin and Savannah. When they'd first met, Savannah was on a mission to infiltrate the company founded by Blake's grandfather to prove that half of King's Finest Distillery belonged to her family. But somehow, they'd managed to move past the pain and distrust to find love and happiness.

Sloane caught the eye of someone on the other side of the room and nodded. She turned back to him. "I'd better go, but we'll catch up later."

"Count on it." Benji watched as she walked away.

Sloane Sutton.

Growing up, he'd adored Sloane. She and his sister, Delia, had been thick as thieves. He'd spent countless nights as a boy kept awake by their girlish giggles, heard through the thin wall between his and Delia's bedrooms. Sloane had been everything to him, but she'd seen him as an honorary little brother.

She'd been a beautiful girl, but she'd grown

into a stunning woman. When they were young, she'd had the toned body of a farm girl who was no stranger to physical labor; her lean, athletic body had given way to softer, fuller curves. The hair she'd worn in a thick, black braid down her back was now cut short on the sides with thick, glossy curls piled atop her head.

A small, barely there diamond stud adorned her left nostril. And when she'd turned to walk away, he'd noticed shooting stars tattooed on the back of her neck. The tattoo disappeared beneath the fabric, which dipped low between her shoulder blades.

"Better close your mouth and stop drooling or everyone will know you've still got a thing for Sloane Sutton," Parker Abbott, his best friend and first cousin, said matter-of-factly.

"I didn't have a *thing* for Sloane Sutton." Benji straightened his navy tuxedo jacket, hoping he wouldn't be struck by lightning for the whopper of a lie he'd just told.

Of course he'd had a thing for Sloane.

He'd been a red-blooded teenage boy and she was…well, she was Sloane Sutton. Confident, beautiful, funny, slightly irreverent.

She hadn't thought him strange because he preferred *Star Trek* marathons and sci-fi books to spending time playing outside. Nor had she ridiculed him for his fascination with computer programming and astronomy or his love of data. Instead, she'd told him how smart he was, and that one day he'd change the world. She'd said it with such confidence, she'd made him believe it, too.

How could he not have had a thing for her?

"I know that reading people isn't my thing," Parker said, "but if *that* wasn't the very definition of having a thing for someone, I'll marry Kayleigh Jemison." He nodded toward the woman he'd escorted down the aisle during the wedding ceremony.

Parker and Kayleigh had been at each other's throats for as long as Benji could remember. But since Kayleigh was close friends with Parker's new sister-in-law, he'd been charged with escorting her down the aisle.

"Speaking of having a thing for someone." Benji chuckled.

"Me? Have a thing for Kayleigh?" Parker's cheeks colored, though he dismissed the idea with a wave of his hand. "You must've fallen and banged your head."

The wedding photographer beckoned them, indicating it was time to join the rest of the wedding party for some group shots.

Benji was thankful for the distraction. Still, he couldn't help scanning the crowd, hoping to catch another glimpse of Sloane.

Sloane nibbled the gloss off her lower lip as she studied Benji from across the room. He took another sip of his beer, then laughed at something Parker said.

She could hardly believe that the incredibly sexy man whose muscular frame filled out his fitted tuxedo in ways that did wicked things to her was the shy, sweet little boy she'd once known.

When his gaze captured hers again, an inexplicable warmth settled low in her belly and her breath caught.

"Are you all right?" Her best friend, Delia, tilted her head. "If I didn't know better, I'd say you were staring at someone at the bar."

Delia turned to look over her shoulder, but

was distracted as her father approached with her daughter in his arms. The two-year-old girl was as beautiful as Delia and generally just as sweet. At this moment, though, she was crying hysterically, demanding her mother.

"Evie, what's wrong, sweetie?" Delia stood, taking her daughter into her arms.

"Your mother says she feels warm." Richard Bennett said. "We were going to offer to take her home with us, but she's insistent that she wants her mama."

"It's okay. Thanks, Dad." Delia kissed the girl's face and she seemed to immediately calm down. She leaned over and kissed Sloane's cheek. "Sorry about this, hon. We'll take up this conversation later. How long will you be in town?"

"I'll probably head back to Nashville tomorrow, but don't worry about me. We'll talk later. Just take care of Evie."

Sloane watched as Delia and Mr. Bennett made their way through the crowd. She sighed, eyeing her half-finished glass of bourbon punch.

With Delia gone, she felt alone—even in a room filled with people she'd known her entire life. Her family and the Abbotts didn't run in the same circles. She just happened to have hit it off with Blake Abbott and his cousin Delia Bennett when they were in grade school. Blake was preoccupied, and Delia was on her way home with little Evie.

There was no reason to stay.

Sloane gulped the rest of her drink, returning the glass to the table with a thud. She stood, bumping into a solid expanse of muscle.

Benji.

He gripped her waist to steady her.

"Sorry, I didn't see you there." She took what she hoped was a subtle step backward. Just out of his reach, but still close enough to savor his provocative scent.

"It was my bad." Benji revealed the sheepish smile that had been his trademark as a kid. He rubbed a hand over his dark brush waves.

Sloane couldn't help smiling, remembering how obsessed Benji had been with perfecting them.

"It was good seeing you again, Benji." Sloane turned to leave, but he placed his strong hand on her arm.

"You're not leaving already, are you? I've been

patiently waiting for a chance to catch up with you. My sister has been monopolizing your time all evening."

"You know how we are when we get together." Sloane smiled. "Not much has changed. We're still basically those same two giggling teenage girls."

"I'd say a lot has changed." Benji's heated gaze drifted down the length of her body, before returning to meet hers.

"I guess you're right." Sloane cleared her throat.

Some things certainly had changed.

Benji had always had a crush on her. There was nothing unusual about a little boy having a crush on his older sister's best friend. Back then, she'd thought it sweet. But Benji Bennett wasn't a little boy anymore. He was a grown-ass man and a fine one at that.

What she saw in his intense dark brown eyes wasn't the misguided admiration of a little boy. It was lust, plain and simple. The same feeling that crawled up her spine and made her heart beat faster.

His confident smile indicated that he could sense her attraction to him.

Pull it together, sister. This is little Benji Bennett you're gawking at here.

Benji had gone to college in Seattle, where he still lived. He'd started his own tech company in his junior year. A company he'd just sold for more than two billion dollars, according to Delia.

Benjamin Bennett was a catch by anyone's standards—even before you factored in his healthy bank account. But he was her best friend's little brother. And though he was all grown up now, he was just a kid, compared to her.

Flirting with Benji would start tongues wagging all over Magnolia Lake. Not that she cared what they thought of her. But her mother and grandfather still lived here. So did Delia, for most of the year. If the whole town started talking, it would make things uncomfortable for the people she loved.

Sloane tore her gaze from his and scanned the room. "I'd better go."

"Don't go. Please. Just one dance." Benji held up a finger, his eyes warm and pleading, his smile sexy and sweet. Then he extended his hand. The same one she'd held when she'd helped him across the street on the way to school when he was five.

Sloane looked at him, then glanced around the space as she nibbled her bottom lip, her heart racing. No one was paying attention to them. The other guests were wrapped up in their own conversations and enjoying the open bar, courtesy of the Abbotts, owners of King's Finest Distillery.

"I guess one dance won't hurt." She placed her hand in his much larger one and let him lead her onto the dance floor.

Benji walked to the center of the dance floor and held her in his arms. He swayed to Jeffrey Osborne's smooth vocals on L.T.D.'s "Love Ballad."

"God, your parents loved this song. They played it so much that your sister and I hated it. Which is a shame, because it's a pretty perfect song."

"It is," he agreed. "You still working for the record company in Nashville?"

"I am. I love what I do, but I've got my eye on a spot on the management team."

"You're the most determined girl I've ever

known." Benji smiled. "If you've set your sights on it, it's as good as done."

"Is that a nice way of calling me stubborn?" It was a familiar put-down from the older folks in town.

"No." His tone was apologetic. "I hated when people said that about you." He sighed softly. "I liked that you were determined. You wanted to move to Nashville and work in the music industry, and that's exactly what you did. I'd say your determination has served you well."

Warmth filled Sloane's chest. Benji had grown up to be extremely wealthy and incredibly handsome, but at his core, he was the same sweet, thoughtful guy she'd always known. His gift for making her smile was still intact.

"Thanks, Benj. That means a lot." Sloane was slightly unnerved by his intense gaze. "Which reminds me, I haven't congratulated you on your big deal." She was eager to turn the conversation away from her. "I should be asking for your autograph. Never met a billionaire before."

The muscles of Benji's back tensed beneath her fingertips and the light in his eyes dimmed.

"I'm the same guy I was before I signed the big deal, Sloane. The same guy I've always been."

"I didn't mean anything by it." She'd only meant to tease him, but she'd struck a nerve instead.

"I know you didn't." He sighed. "I'm just a little fed up with people treating me differently. You wouldn't believe how many obscure business ideas I've been pitched tonight."

She hadn't considered that there might be a downside to becoming a multibillionaire. But for her, never having to worry about how she'd pay second mortgages on her condo and their family farm would outweigh the disadvantages. "I'm sorry you've had to deal with that."

"Don't apologize. You're just about the only unattached woman in the room who doesn't see me as a golden lottery ticket." He nodded toward the gaggle of women in the corner of the room, whispering to one another and staring at him. "Not one of them would've given me the time of day back then. Their only interest in me was whether I could hook them up with one of my wealthy cousins. Now they've been stalking me all night. But you—I had to beg you to dance with me."

A knot tightened in her stomach. She had a good job and owned a cute little condo that she was slowly renovating in one of the hottest neighborhoods in Nashville. But she was in debt up to her eyeballs. Not because she was a frivolous spender addicted to retail therapy, but because she'd sunk every penny of her savings into helping her mother save their family farm. Then there were the bills that had been piling up since her grandfather's costly heart surgery.

Her budget was so tight it had practically squealed when she'd purchased the fancy dress she was wearing, despite finding it on the clearance rack at a designer dress shop.

If there was one thing she'd learned from her grandfather, Atticus Ames, it was pride. She'd work three jobs and sell plasma before she'd ask Benji or anyone else in this town for a handout.

"I told you that one day they'd regret ignoring you." Sloane grinned. She honestly couldn't have been prouder of Benji if he'd been her own flesh and blood.

"You did." A soft smile played across his hand-

some face. "I was an awkward kid trying to figure out my place in life. But you always made
me feel that just being me was good enough. You
said that everyone else was just slow to catch up.
That eventually they'd figure it out. You made
me believe it, too."

Sloane's heart swelled. She was moved by his
confession. "You were a special kid, destined
for great things. I always knew that. And look
at you… You've exceeded my wildest expecta-
tions."

He smiled, looking bashful, yet deliciously
handsome. Her heart beat a little faster; she
needed to change the subject.

"Evie's gotten so big, and she looks just like
Delia. I'm surprised your parents aren't urging
you to settle down and give them more grandchildren."

"You know them well." Benji grinned. "My
mother sneaks it into the conversation whenever
she can. Don't get me wrong. Evie's a cool kid
and everything, but 3:00 a.m. feedings and dirty
diapers just aren't for me."

Sloane understood exactly how Benji felt. The
primary reason her ex had filed for divorce was

because he was ready to start a family but she wasn't. Though, truth be told, it was just one of the many reasons their marriage had failed.

"What about you? Are Davis and Evie giving you baby fever, too?" Benji teased.

"Me?" She forced a laugh. "Between rehabbing my condo and being completely focused on my career, I forget to feed myself most days."

True. Still, holding little Davis, with his chubby little legs and sweet baby scent, made her think for the briefest moment about one day having a baby of her own. A thought she dismissed immediately.

Finally, the song ended.

"Thanks for the dance." Sloane slipped out of Benji's embrace, determined to banish the inappropriate thoughts that had commandeered her brain and made her body ache for the warmth and comfort of his strong arms.

Benji lowered their joined hands but didn't let go. Instead, he leaned down, his lips brushing her ear and his well-trimmed beard gently scraping her neck. "Let's get out of here."

It was a bad idea. A *really* bad idea.

Her cheeks burned. "But it's your cousin's wedding."

He nodded toward Blake, who was dancing with his bride, Savannah, as their infant son slept on his shoulder. The man was in complete bliss.

"I doubt he'll notice I'm gone. Besides, you'd be rescuing me. If Jeb Dawson tells me one more time about his latest invention—"

"Okay, okay." Sloane held back a giggle as she glanced around the room. "You need to escape as badly as I do. But there's no way we're leaving here together. It'd be on the front page of the newspaper by morning."

"Valid point." Benji chuckled. "So meet me at the cabin."

"The cabin on the lake?" She had so many great memories of weekends spent there with Delia and her family.

"My parents hardly used it after they bought their place in Florida. I bought it from them a few years ago and Cole completely rehabbed it. I'd love for you to see it."

Just two old friends catching up on each other's lives. Nothing wrong with that.

She repeated it three times in her head. But

there was nothing *friendly* about the sensations that danced along her spine when he'd held her in his arms and pinned her with that piercing gaze.

"Okay. Maybe we can catch up over a cup of coffee or something."

"Or something." The corner of his sensuous mouth curved in a smirk. A shiver ran through her as she wondered, for the briefest moment, how his lips would taste. "Meet you there in half an hour."

He disappeared into the crowd, leaving her missing his warmth.

Benji made two more cups of coffee and added creamer to Sloane's before setting the cup in front of her.

She thanked him and reached for her cup. But her eyes widened when she caught a glimpse of the time, flashing on her fitness watch when she flipped her wrist. "I didn't realize it was so late. You must be exhausted, and I'm keeping you up."

"You can't possibly think I want you to go." Benji placed his hand on hers. "The last two hours were the best time I've had since I've been back in town."

"Me, too." Sloane smiled. A deep, genuine smile. Then she frowned, a crease forming between her brows as she slipped her hand from beneath his. She stood abruptly, smoothing her dress over her hips. "Which is why I should go."

Benji stood, too, his eyes searching Sloane's. For the first time in his life, Sloane Sutton wasn't treating him like a little boy with a crush. Tonight, she saw him as a man. A man she desired.

He could see the passion in her brown eyes. Feel the heat that had been building between them all night.

When he was ten years old, he'd decided he was in love with Sloane because she was the nicest, prettiest girl he knew.

The passage of fifteen years hadn't altered his opinion. With her standing this close, her luscious scent washing over him, his boyhood conviction was reinforced.

He wanted to be with this woman. To hold her in his arms. To tease every inch of her gorgeous body. Make love to her.

Get her out of his system once and for all, so he could stop living in the past.

They hadn't seen each other in ten years. And

in three days he'd be boarding a flight to Japan for the six-month-long consulting gig he'd agreed to when he sold his company. When it was over, he'd return to Seattle and Sloane would be back home in Nashville. Who knew when they'd see each other again?

Speak now, Benj, or forever hold your peace.

Benji stepped closer, his gaze locked with Sloane's. She inhaled audibly, her body tensing as he leaned down and cradled her face. The sound of Sloane breathing and the frantic beat of his heart filled his ears.

Sloane didn't object to the intimate gesture. Her pupils dilated, and her chest rose and fell heavily. He moved in closer, and she leaned in, too. She pressed a hand to his chest and her eyes drifted shut.

He kissed her, easing into it at first, reveling in the softness of her lips and the way her body nestled against his. Her lips parted on a sigh, granting his tongue access. Her mouth tasted rich and sweet. Like premium bourbon and pecan pie.

As the urgency of his kiss escalated, Sloane's response matched his intensity.

Eager. Hungry. Demanding.

His heart thundered in his chest, his need for her building. He hauled her closer and groaned with pleasure at the sensation of his length pinned between them.

Sloane slipped her arms around him and tugged his shirt free from the back of his pants. Her fingernails scraped gently against his skin.

Benji groaned, hardening painfully as the sensation—part pain, part pleasure—heightened the euphoric feeling that vibrated beneath his skin. Made him desperate to finally have her. He lifted her onto the table, nestling in the space between her thighs.

He swallowed her gasp in response to the sudden move, kissing her harder. Losing himself in the clash of lips and tongues and the delicious sensation of their bodies moving against each other, desperate for more contact than their clothing would permit.

He savored her intoxicating scent and relished the feel of her full breasts with their hardened peaks pressed against his chest.

She glided her fingertips down his stomach and fumbled with his belt buckle, loosening it.

"You have no idea how long I've been waiting for this," he whispered, his lips brushing her ear.

Sloane's hands froze. Her eyes opened and her gaze had shifted from one of intense desire to one of regret.

"Hey, beautiful." Benji traced her cheekbone with his thumb. "Did I say something wrong?"

"I shouldn't have come here, and we shouldn't be doing this." She lowered her gaze.

He was seconds away from making his boyhood fantasy a reality and he'd blown it, because he couldn't keep his stupid mouth shut.

Way to go, Benj.

"Why not?" He spoke calmly, trying to put her at ease. "We're consenting adults."

"I've known you since you were five. You're my best friend's little brother. I've introduced you as *my* little brother." She shook her head, her eyes still not meeting his. "This is bad. What would Delia say? And what would your parents think?"

"My mother will never believe anyone is good enough, and my sister adores you." Benji dropped a slow, lingering kiss on her lips.

"Because I'm her friend, who she trusts not to

blow into town and screw her little brother." She jabbed him in the gut, but her lips parted to his tongue when he kissed her again.

"You're too young for me, Benji," she whispered against his lips as he slid the silky, blue material down her shoulder.

He kissed the shell of her ear. "Five years mattered then. It doesn't now."

"I'm not looking for a relationship, Benj." She pressed her hands to his chest, halting his movement as her gaze met his. Still, she hadn't moved an inch. Her legs framed his as she awaited his response.

"Neither am I," he said finally. "That doesn't mean we can't be together. I want you, Sloane. And I know you want me, too." He slowly tugged the zipper down her back. The silky, cobalt blue material slid from her shoulders, giving him better access. He trailed kisses down her shoulder and across the top of her breasts, exposed by a pale pink strapless bra. "Just for tonight."

She sucked in a deep breath and let the material slip down her arms and pool around her waist. Sloane unbuttoned his pants and inched the zipper down. The sound echoed off the solid oak floors and shiplap walls. She leaned in to kiss him. "Just for tonight."

Usually an early riser, Benji refused to leave the warmth of Sloane's curves. Her naked bottom was nestled against him, making him painfully hard. Which gave him hope they'd pick up where they'd left off just a few hours earlier when sleep had finally pulled them under.

Starting at her neck, he planted gentle kisses to the shooting stars that tattooed the length of her spine. By the time he reached the stars inked between her shoulder blades, she stirred.

"Mmm. Nice way to wake a girl."

He rolled her, so she was facing him. Her pebbled brown nipples betrayed her arousal. "I can think of an even better way to wake you."

"Bathroom first," she mumbled through the hand clamped over her mouth.

"Anything you need is in there." He nodded toward the adjoining bathroom before dropping another kiss on her shoulder. "Just hurry back."

When Sloane returned, he was seated with his back propped against the padded leather headboard. Her bashful smile slowly gave way to a determined one. Her eyes locked with his as she straddled him. Bracing her hands on his shoulders, she leaned in and kissed him, tentatively at first.

He fought the urge to take over. Instead, he let her dictate the pace and manage the heat building between them. Sloane palmed his face and angled her head, her tongue gliding against his and her slick folds gliding along his heated flesh. She swiveled her hips, the pace and intensity of her movements more frantic.

Benji groaned with pleasure, losing all sense of control as he dug his fingers into the soft skin at her hip that bore a mandala tattoo with a rose at its center. He jerked her hips forward and then back. They were both getting closer to the edge, and he ached with the need to be inside her again. He flipped them over, so he lay atop her, and reached into the nightstand for a foil packet, fumbling to put it on.

He was desperate to get his fill of the woman who'd haunted his dreams since puberty. The only woman he'd ever really wanted.

Sloane wrapped her legs around him as he moved inside her. Her fingernails dug into his shoulders and her breath caught as she flew apart beneath him. His name rolled off her tongue as her muscles tensed, pulling him beneath the river of pleasure that washed over them.

Benji tumbled to the mattress, his skin slick with sweat and his breathing labored. He pulled her to him and kissed her damp forehead. "Come to Japan with me, Sloane."

The words he'd whispered impulsively into her hair took him by surprise. They'd agreed to one night together, not a six-month-long commitment. *Smooth, Benj.*

His brain urged him to revoke the invitation. But everything below his neck desperately wanted her to say yes.

"Sure. It'll be a blast. We can eat sushi every day, sing karaoke every night and ride the bullet train on the weekends. Besides, seeing the cherry blossoms in bloom is on my bucket list. Just give me a few hours to throw a travel bag together."

"You'll come with me?" Abject terror and genuine excitement battled in his chest. The way they did during the seconds when a roller coaster made its painfully slow ascent to the summit before plummeting toward the earth.

"Wait…" Sloane lifted her head from his chest and blinked, her head cocked. "You're not serious, are you?"

His shoulders tensed. "Dead serious."

"Benji, I can't. I thought you understood that this was just…"

"A game?"

"Fun. A release. Two people being a little naughty for the weekend." Sloane pulled the sheet around her, suddenly self-conscious. She sat up, her back against the headboard. "But us getting serious? That can't happen. I thought you were clear on that."

"I am, and that doesn't have to change. But it was nice to wake up to someone who made me want to spend the day in bed." He shrugged. "I haven't had that in a long time."

"Neither have I, but—"

"Then why not keep doing it? In Japan," he added.

Sloane dragged her fingers through her messy curls and huffed. "And while you're working every day, what am I supposed to do? Lounge around, waiting for my sugar daddy to get home? No thanks, Benj. I'm not interested in being anyone's kept woman. Not even a billionaire's." She climbed out of bed, taking the sheet with her as she wrapped it around her body and rummaged on the floor for her bra and panties. "Besides, I have a job and responsibilities, and I don't have a passport. Never needed one."

Benji dragged the remaining covers up to his waist. "I wasn't thinking of the arrangement that way at all. We'd just be two friends hanging out."

"And screwing. On your dime." She looked at him pointedly. "Plus, you just called it 'an arrangement.' So if it looks like a duck and it quacks like a duck—"

She had a point.

He had just turned into *that* guy. The one who thought he could buy anyone and anything. Even the woman he adored.

"Point taken." He cleared his throat. "Like I said, that wasn't my intention."

"I know it wasn't. And I'm flattered you asked." Her tone and her gaze softened. She gripped her blue dress to her chest as she approached him and brushed a soft kiss to his lips. "If the situation was different..." Sloane wouldn't allow herself to finish the thought.

It was just as well. No point in musing about some alternate universe in which she would say yes.

Benji did the only thing there was left to do. He tugged her to him. Her dress tumbled to the floor, quickly joined by the pale pink bra and panties.

One

Six months later

Benji inhaled the scent of the roses, lilies and snapdragons overflowing his arms as he approached Sloane's building.

The edge of his mouth curled in a faint smile. Sloane had always loved the scent of the snapdragons his mother grew in their front yard.

He halted in front of the red door and drew in a deep breath.

It's just friends going out for coffee. No big deal.

At least that was the first step of his grand plan. He'd invite her to coffee where they could have a discussion on neutral ground about the possibility of picking up where they'd left off before he'd departed for Japan.

He'd casually inquired about Sloane during his absence, but his sister had been unusually tight-lipped about her friend, so he didn't press. It would only raise his sister's suspicions about why he was so interested.

So he'd simply told Delia that he needed Sloane's address for his Christmas list. Not a lie, but not the primary reason he was asking.

Benji had considered picking up the phone and calling Sloane while he was in Japan. But she'd been so adamant that walking away was the right thing to do. There was no way he would've been able to persuade her with a long-distance phone call.

He'd kept himself busy with work, but when it was time to book his flight home, he realized he'd arrive on Valentine's Day.

It had seemed like a sign.

So instead of flying directly to Seattle, he'd booked a flight to Nashville. He needed to speak to Sloane in person.

Maybe he was crazy to believe there could be

anything more between them. But dealing with Sloane's rejection would be a lot less painful than suffering a lifetime of regret.

Clutching the flower arrangement in one arm, he rang Sloane's buzzer.

"You looking for Sloane?" The woman in the unit across from Sloane's peered down from the balcony where she was sweeping. "She left a couple of hours ago, but if you have a delivery for her, I'll sign for it."

"Thank you." Benji tried not to sound as defeated as he felt. "But Sloane's an old family friend. I was hoping to deliver these in person."

"Then you're in luck." The older woman pointed toward a vehicle that had just turned down the lane next to the building. "That's her truck pulling around back."

Benji thanked the woman and made his way behind the building. Sloane had parked her car in the garage and was rummaging in her trunk.

He approached her silently, still replaying in his head exactly what he planned to say. Gripping the flowers in one arm, Benji stopped a few feet short of where she stood. He shoved his free hand in his pocket.

"Hey, Sloane."

"Benji?" Her body stiffened, and she glanced over her shoulder. "What are you doing here?"

Not the reception he'd hoped for. He forced a smile anyway.

"I wanted to surprise you for Valentine's Day. I thought that, if you don't already have plans, maybe we could do something together." He cleared his throat when she still hadn't turned around. "I flew straight here from Japan because I really needed to see you."

"You shouldn't have come." She turned back to the groceries in her trunk. "This isn't what we agreed to."

"I know it isn't, but—"

"You should go. Now. Please." She arranged the grocery bags in her trunk into two rows, her back to him.

"Can't we at least talk about this?" He hated that he sounded like a kid negotiating his bed-time with the babysitter. He was a grown man. A business owner. A self-made fucking billionaire whose business advice was in demand.

So why did he revert to a love-struck little boy whenever he was around Sloane?

"No." Sloane stood up straight, abruptly smacking her head on the raised deck lid. She swayed, her body going limp.

"Sloane!" Benji dropped the flowers to the ground and surged forward, catching her before she hit the concrete.

"I've got you." He hoisted her into his arms. She was noticeably heavier than she'd been when he'd carried her to his bed six months ago.

Is that why she didn't want to see him? Was she self-conscious about her weight gain? She should know him well enough to realize that would never matter to him.

"Sloane. Sloane! Honey, are you all right?" His heart beat faster.

She was breathing but unresponsive.

Benji carried her to the passenger side of her car and put her in the seat to drive her to the hospital. He stretched the seat belt to put it over her, his gaze trailing down to her burgeoning belly.

"Sloane, you're… I mean…are you—"

"Pregnant?" The word came out as more of a moan as her eyes fluttered open. One hand moved to her belly and rubbed it in a soothing circle. "Yes."

"Exactly how pregnant are you?"

"Very." Sloane forced a weak laugh, then winced. When he didn't react, she cleared her throat and her expression grew serious, too. Her response was little more than a whisper. "Six months."

"Is it… I mean…am I…" He felt as if he were suffocating, unable to get the words out. He swallowed hard and tried again. "Is the baby mine?"

"I haven't been with anyone but you since my divorce, so my money is on you. I'm not really the immaculate conception type."

He narrowed his gaze at Sloane. How could she joke about the fact that he was going to be a father in just a few months and she hadn't even had the decency to let him know. "Were you ever going to tell me?"

"Honestly? I don't know." The sarcasm she'd been using as a shield evaporated, and he noticed that the corners of her eyes were suddenly damp. Her gaze didn't meet his. "That weekend, you made it pretty clear that you weren't the daddy type."

"What do you—" He stopped midsentence, recalling their conversation about his niece.

Evie's a cool kid and everything, but 3:00 a.m. feedings and dirty diapers just aren't for me.

"I was speaking in hypotheticals. As in, I had no immediate plans to have children. Not as in, I'm such a coldhearted bastard that I wouldn't want to know my own baby."

"Babies." Sloane emphasized the *s* at the end of the word as she reached up and rubbed the spot where the lid of the trunk had tagged her head. She grimaced.

"Twins?" Benji's voice reverted to the high pitch of a boy entering puberty. He cleared his throat and tried again. "We're having twins?"

Benji's gaze returned to her belly. For a moment he felt weak. As if everything was spinning around them.

"*I'm* having twins." Sloane's voice deepened as she gripped her belly and winced. "Hopefully not at this moment. It's too soon, but something doesn't feel right."

Benji felt the knot rising on her head, then touched her stomach, but drew his hand back. Despite everything they'd done that weekend, the simple act of touching her belly suddenly felt intrusive. Too intimate.

"I'm getting you to a doctor." He stretched the seat belt across her body and secured it, then demanded her keys.

She stared at him as if she wanted to give him the finger, but she reached into her pocket instead, and handed him the keys without a word.

Benji retrieved the bouquet he'd brought for Sloane from the ground and got into the driver's seat.

"Those are for me, I presume." Her voice was softer. Apologetic.

"Oh, yeah. Here." He handed her the flowers that looked the worse for wear after he'd clenched them in a Vulcan death grip and then dropped them to keep her from falling. "Happy Valentine's Day," he mumbled bitterly.

"Snapdragons." She whispered the word as she inhaled their scent. Suddenly tears were running down her face.

"Are you in pain?" He gripped her arm.

"Yes, but that isn't why I'm crying." She sniffled. "It's these stupid hormones and…" She sniffled again, louder this time. "You remembered that I like snapdragons."

Benji sighed and gave her a pained smile despite the anger that was burning inside his chest. "I remember everything about you, Sloane. No matter how damn hard I've tried to forget."

Benji's words hurt.

More than the physical discomfort of one of the twins bouncing on her bladder while her belly felt as if it was being squeezed in a vise.

He'd tried to forget her. Meanwhile, Benji had been all she could think of even before she'd learned she was pregnant—with twins, no less.

Because when she screwed up, she did it big.

She'd spent the two months after their night together regretting that she hadn't taken him up on his offer to join him in Japan, daydreaming about their incredible night together and wanting him. She'd been so preoccupied with work and thoughts of Benji that she hadn't noticed that she'd missed not one but two periods. Until the sudden, severe case of morning sickness she developed made it clear she was pregnant.

"I'm sorry you had to find out like this." Sloane stared out the window, not wanting to see the hatred and disappointment in his eyes.

"Why didn't you tell me?" His words vibrated with hurt and anger. Pain.

"I know I should've, but…" She turned toward him, needing to see that he was okay. She licked her lips, her throat incredibly dry. "This isn't what you signed up for. We agreed to a one-night stand, not an eighteen-year commitment as parents. Besides, you made it pretty clear that kids weren't something you wanted."

"I was speaking in generalities, Sloane." He clenched the wheel as he turned a corner.

"You said, and I quote—"

"I'm aware of what I said. I remember everything that happened between us that night." He took another sharp turn, following the directions of the GPS app. "But how could you think that meant I wouldn't take care of my own flesh and blood, or wouldn't want to know that I have a son or daughter somewhere out in the world?"

"It's both." She winced again, pressing a hand to her belly, trying to calm herself as the pain got worse. "A boy and a girl."

He glanced at her quickly before returning his gaze to the road. "Does this happen often? The pain, I mean?"

"Not like this." Tears stung her eyes, more from fear than from the pain. It was too early for the twins to be born. Not if they were going to be okay. She forced a laugh. "Usually it's just discomfort from your son bouncing his big head on my bladder and your daughter doing some kind of calisthenics. I swear, that girl is going to be a gymnast."

"Everything is gonna be okay." He reached over and squeezed her hand, despite the reserved anger in his tone. "First, we make sure you and the babies are all right. Then…"

"I'll tell you anything you want to know," she said, grateful to see the hospital sign come into view. "I promise."

Benji hadn't stopped pacing outside Sloane's hospital room since they'd admitted her.

He was going to be a father of two babies—a boy and a girl. He still couldn't wrap his head around it. He'd been responsible and used protection every time they were together.

How could this have happened?

Benji's phone vibrated in his pocket and he glanced at the screen. It was his mother. Probably checking to see if he'd returned safely from Japan. But he didn't dare answer the call. Not yet. Not until he'd gotten some definitive answers from Sloane about why she hadn't told him he was going to be a father. Regardless of what he'd said that night, he couldn't believe that was the only reason Sloane had kept something this important from him.

He respected the fact that it was Sloane who was carrying these babies, but they were half his, too. What about his right to know? And to be part of his children's lives? Sloane's father had left home when she was around ten. She understood the pain of living without a father. Why would she intentionally subject their kids to the same fate?

The door opened, and the doctor introduced herself and invited him into the room where Sloane was hooked up to an IV. She gave him an apologetic smile before lowering her gaze to her hands, which were pressed to her belly.

"Is Sloane okay? Will the twins be all right?" he asked Dr. Carroll.

The older woman placed a gentle hand on his arm. "Sloane is going to be just fine, Mr. Bennett. She's experiencing something called Braxton Hicks contractions. It's basically the uterus practicing up for child labor." Her smile deepened. "They're usually painless, but Sloane is experiencing particularly intense ones today. She's dehydrated. That likely contributed to it."

He nodded dumbly, his hands shaking and his head feeling light. None of this seemed real.

"Perhaps you should have a seat." Worry lines spanned the doctor's forehead as she indicated a sofa along the wall. She sat beside him. "Just take a deep breath. I realize this must seem very overwhelming, but everything is going to be fine."

"Sorry, this is all kind of a surprise."

"I know." The woman nodded gravely. "Sloane explained the situation to me. I can only imagine what a shock it must've been. But the good news is, you have the opportunity to be there for the birth of your children. And you and Sloane still have lots of time before the twins are born to hash things out." She looked pointedly at both of them in a firm but kind manner. "The twins are counting on you two to do that."

"Will she be released today?" Benji wasn't

ready to talk about making nice. Not until he got some straight answers.

"I want to observe her for another hour. But as long as everything looks good, yes, she can go home. This isn't preterm labor, but I still want her to take it easy." The woman shifted her gaze to Sloane, and her tone and expression turned more serious. "Make sure she understands my instructions that she refrain from working. That includes not hauling groceries around. If she can't comply with my limited restrictions, I'll have to put her on full bed rest."

"I understand," Sloane said, her expression contrite. "I would never knowingly put the babies in jeopardy."

"I know you wouldn't, Sloane. But you're carrying multiples. That makes everything a little trickier. So let's err on the side of caution." Dr. Carroll moved beside Sloane and squeezed her arm briefly before making a few notes on the tablet in her hand and checking the monitor.

"Any other specific things she shouldn't be doing?" Benji was on his feet beside the doctor.

"Nothing strenuous. No lifting or high-impact exercise. Walking, swimming and gentle yoga should be okay." She turned to Sloane. "But you should monitor how you're feeling. Make sure there's no pain or unusual discomfort." She turned back to Benji with a sly smile. "And there are no restrictions on sex, within reason. If that's what you're asking."

Benji's cheeks heated and he sputtered, "No, that isn't what I was asking."

"Relax, Benj." Sloane and the doctor were laughing. "I have no intention of jumping you when we get back to my place."

Benji glared at her, not acknowledging her jab. He returned his attention to the doctor. "I was referring to the bump she took to the head. She passed out momentarily. Does she have a concussion? Will it impact the twins?"

"Relax, Mr. Bennett." Dr. Carroll's voice was patient and soothing. Like she was trying to convince a man in a straitjacket that he hadn't been abducted by aliens. "She has a little knot there, but no concussion. We applied an ice pack to reduce the swelling. Something she should continue to do off and on this evening. But if she suddenly seems woozy or disoriented, by all means, bring her back."

"Will the Braxton Hicks contractions always be this strong?" Sloane asked. Her voice was strained, the levity gone.

Benji quickly made his way over to Sloane and let her grip his hand. It seemed to ease her discomfort.

When he looked up at the doctor she was smiling, seemingly pleased by his instinctive need to comfort Sloane.

"If you stay hydrated, knock off strenuous activities and reduce your stress levels, hopefully they won't be as intense. In fact, you might not feel them at all." Dr. Carroll turned to Benji. "If they do become intense, give her fluids and get her to walk around a little. That should relieve them."

The woman handed him a pamphlet from her pocket. "I went over this with Sloane earlier. It outlines the difference between Braxton Hicks contractions and preterm labor—which can be dangerous for the babies at this stage. Study it. Memorize it. We want these babies to gestate until at least thirty-seven weeks, if possible."

"Benji doesn't live here. He'll be going back to Seattle," Sloane interjected.

"No, I won't. I'm not leaving your side until the twins are born. Not up for discussion," he added, glaring at her again when she opened her mouth to object.

She snapped her mouth shut and rubbed her belly.

"Good." Dr. Carroll nodded approvingly. "Because she's been trying to do this on her own for too long, and I've been worried about her."

Benji couldn't help the twinge of guilt in his gut at the doctor's remarks, despite the fact that he couldn't possibly have known that Sloane was struggling through this pregnancy on her own. The guilt quickly turned to resentment.

He should've been there, and he would've been, if only Sloane had given him the courtesy of a single phone call or even a text message.

"All right, I don't expect to see you again until your next *scheduled* visit at the office." Dr. Carroll raised one brow at Sloane before turning to Benji. "Walk me out, Mr. Bennett?"

He followed the woman into the hall.

"I know you must be angry and that you have many questions for Sloane." She pinned him with her piercing blue eyes. "I don't begrudge you for that. But she doesn't need any unnecessary stress. So keep that in mind as you search for answers and you two decide what comes next. Capisce?"

"Yes, ma'am." He nodded, shoving his hands in his pockets.

"Good." Her expression softened. She patted his arm. "Give her a chance to explain. And listen to all the things she's afraid to say. She's one tough lady, but deep down she's terrified of going through this alone. So don't let her fool you into believing that she doesn't want or need your help." Dr. Carroll reached out to shake Benji's hand. "You two take care of each other and the two little people growing inside her."

Benji sighed and nodded. "We'll figure it out."

When he returned to Sloane's room, she immediately tensed, her eyes not meeting his.

Benji sucked in a deep breath and pulled a chair up beside Sloane. He sat back in the chair. "Okay, let's talk."

Two

Sloane's heart felt as if it were beating out of her chest. And despite all the water she'd been made to drink in the short time since she'd been admitted, it felt like she was swallowing sand.

Her hands shook, and it took everything she had to maintain his gaze.

He was angry and hurt. Disappointed. In her.

So different from what she'd felt when she'd stared into those brooding brown eyes six months ago.

Her reasons for not telling Benji about the pregnancy seemed honorable and self-sacrificing when she'd made the decision to keep it from him. But now, faced with his resentment, they felt like cowardly excuses to avoid this very moment. When she'd have to face him again.

"I didn't do this to hurt you, Benji. I honestly thought I was doing you a favor by keeping you out of the mess that I've made."

"It's not like you did this alone. I distinctly remember being there, too." He folded his arms.

A wave of heat came over her and her nipples prickled with the memory of what had happened between them that weekend. How he'd made her feel.

"So why in the—" He drew in a deep breath and closed his eyes for a moment. She could swear he was counting to ten under his breath. Finally he opened them again and released a long sigh. "So why on earth would you think you needed to handle this on your own?"

"Because I'm not twentysomething anymore. I'm old enough to know better. I should never have gone to your cabin that night. Never let you kiss me." Sloane shook her head, tears sliding down her cheeks. *Damn hormones.* She wiped away the tears with the back of one trembling fist.

"I'm not nine, Sloane." His voice was softer,

though it still vibrated with controlled anger. "I don't need you to cover for me like you did when I broke Mom's favorite vase." A faint smile momentarily curled the edges of his mouth. "You don't need to shield me from the consequences of my actions. And money, obviously, isn't an issue. I can take care of you and the babies."

"That's just it…" The pain rising in her gut had nothing to do with the Braxton Hicks contractions and everything to do with the rumors that had swirled around Magnolia Lake her entire life. "Everyone back home will swear I got knocked up on purpose. That this was all some grand plan to secure my family's future by having a billionaire's baby."

"I know Magnolia Lake still feels like a little backwoods town." He practically snorted. "But even they understand how babies are made."

"I'm not joking, Benj." She rubbed her belly. "You don't understand because…" Sloane shook her head and lay back on the pillow, staring up at the ceiling. "Never mind."

"No, tell me." He sat on the edge of his chair. "You say I don't understand, so school me on why rational adults would completely ignore my role in this and blame you."

"They'll say, like mother like daughter." Tears burned her eyes. Her life in Magnolia Lake seemed like a lifetime ago. Yet, the pain of that phrase uttered underneath folks' breath still hurt.

Benji was quiet, as if he suddenly remembered the cruel things folks in town had said about her and her mother. He cleared his throat. "You're not your mom, Sloane. No matter what they say—"

"What they say about her isn't true."

Sloane met his gaze. She didn't always get along with Abigail Sutton. Nor had she completely gotten over her resentment of her mother. But no one else got to talk shit about her. Especially when what they were saying was a bald-faced lie.

Sloane sat up in the bed and adjusted her pillows. "She didn't 'trick' my father into marrying her. She was young and stupid enough to believe he actually loved her. She was too naive to understand that the Suttons would never approve of a poor girl from the wrong side of town."

"Look, Sloane, I'm sorry for what a few busybodies might've said to make you feel that you were somehow inferior. But we both know that isn't true. I've never believed it. Nor does my family."

She wanted to tell him she knew his mother had never liked her. It was obvious from the coldness in her voice and in her eyes, despite the fake smile she always managed for Sloane's benefit. Constance Bennett had merely tolerated her, preferring that she and Delia spend time at their home, under her careful supervision.

But there was no point in reopening old wounds when there were fresh ones gushing bright red blood that needed tending.

"You have to admit, it'll seem odd that you returned to Magnolia Lake a billionaire and suddenly I'm having your babies. Then there's our age difference." She pressed a palm to her suddenly throbbing right eye. "Your sister is going to kill me."

"Forget everyone else for a minute. This isn't about any of them. It's about me and you and…" His gaze was drawn to her belly before he raised it to hers again. "Our babies." He swallowed hard, leaning closer. "Do you mind if… I mean, would it be all right if—"

Her heart swelled with affection for this man.

The sheepish look on his face as he struggled to ask for permission to touch her after the intimacy they'd shared that night was utterly adorable.

"Give me your hand." She reached out for his, guiding it to her belly between the two straps from the electronic fetal monitor that crossed her midsection. "Put your hand here."

"I don't feel any—"

"Shh…" She closed her eyes, her voice lowered. "Just wait."

They sat still, his hand on her stomach. The only sound in the room was the intermittent beeping of the IV pump.

Suddenly one of the babies kicked. Sloane smiled when she opened her eyes and saw the look of amazement on Benji's face.

"I can't believe it. I could really feel that. That's incredible." His voice broke slightly. "That's my…*our* baby."

Her chest tightened at his use of the phrase. She'd only ever thought of the babies as *hers*.

"That was your son." Sloane adjusted her position as the baby kicked again. "I don't know what my ribs ever did to him, but he's got it out for them."

No longer tentative, Benji pressed more firmly on the area where he'd felt the kick. He jumped, startled as the skin high on her belly shifted. Their baby girl started to roll.

"It's okay. The first time I saw that, I was pretty weirded out, too." She smiled so much her cheeks hurt. "Looked like something straight out of one of your favorite sci-fi movies."

That seemed to relax him a little. Benji glided his hand to where her skin stretched and moved. He touched what looked like a tiny little shoulder. It protruded slightly from her belly, then disappeared from sight again.

He stood, staring at her stomach in awe for a few moments before he met her eyes again.

"I wasn't around during most of my sister's pregnancy, so I didn't see any of that." He indicated her belly. "It really is remarkable."

"Speaking of remarkable—" she pointed a thumb over her shoulder at the electronic fetal monitor "—I asked Dr. Carroll to turn the sound off before you came in the room. Turn that dial up."

Benji went to the machine and turned up the volume. His eyes sparked with recognition as he turned to meet her gaze again. "That's a heart-beat." He listened carefully, turning the volume up a little more. "No, it's two heartbeats."

She rubbed her stomach again. "That's right."

Benji dragged a hand over his head and sat beside the bed. His brows furrowed as the pain and disappointment returned to his face, forming hardened lines that weren't there before. "How could you not tell me?"

Sloane's phone rang. She swiped it from the table beside her bed, thankful for a respite from the withering heat of Benji's stare.

Mama.

Sloane hadn't thought to call her mother. But the last thing she wanted was to give her mom an excuse to come to Nashville and set up camp at her place. With her growing belly and all of the baby things she was collecting in duplicate, the place already felt too small.

She silenced the phone and turned it facedown. She'd return the call once she was settled in back at her place. No need to worry her mother un-necessarily.

There was nothing to tell.

Except that the man her mother still referred

to as "little Benji Bennett" was the father of her babies. And that wasn't a conversation she was prepared to have.

"Everything okay?" Deep worry lines creased his forehead.

"Everything's fine." She pulled the sheet around her and asked him to turn down the monitor again. "Now, about what you said when Dr. Carroll was in here."

"About me not returning to Seattle?" He raised a brow and narrowed his gaze.

"Yes, that." She refused to repeat the words that both terrified her and made her hopeful. "That isn't necessary. As Dr. Carroll explained, there's nothing wrong with me or the babies."

"I missed the first six months of your pregnancy. I'm not missing another minute."

It wasn't a question or even a suggestion.

"You've pretty much gotten the highlights. The first two months, I had no idea I was pregnant. Then there was four months of barfing my brains out before the morning sickness finally subsided." She settled back against the pillow.

"The morning sickness was that bad?"

"It bordered on spectacular. I had acute morning sickness, which, by the way, is a misnomer. There was nothing cute about not being able to hold down anything or work for the past four months."

A pained look crimped Benji's face. "You've been out of work for four months? How've you been paying your expenses?"

Sloane's cheeks stung with embarrassment. Her dire financial situation wasn't a conversation she wanted to have with the golden boy billionaire. She'd gotten herself into this mess and it was her job to navigate her way out of it. If there was one thing she'd learned in her thirty years, it was that when she got into difficulty, no one was coming to rescue her. She needed to figure this out on her own, just as she'd done her entire life.

"Sloane?" he prodded.

"I manage." She stared down at her ragged fingernails and fought the urge to chew on them.

Benji spoke after a few moments of awkward silence between them. "When you were filling out the hospital paperwork… I couldn't help noticing the past-due bills hanging out of your wallet."

"You snooped in my purse?" The heat in her cheeks turned to a butane-lighter-charged flame.

"I wasn't snooping. I just couldn't help noticing the words stamped in bold red capital letters." He raised his hands in self-defense, then sighed. "Sloane, what are you trying to prove? I have all this money. What good is it if I can't even help the people I care about?"

"That's not what you said at the reception." She folded her arms and glared at him pointedly. "You said you were tired of people treating you differently. Like you were a freakin' ATM. I couldn't bear for you, Delia or your parents to ever think I'm no better than the girls who stalked you at the wedding. That I looked at you and got dollar signs in my eyes. That I planned this to ensure I'd get a big ol' piece of the Benji Bennett pie."

"Sloane, no one will think that."

"I've been taking care of myself since I was sixteen. I worked a job, in addition to my duties on the farm. Paid my own way. I've never needed to ask anyone for anything." Tears formed in her eyes again. She swiped at them, but that didn't stop fresh tears from falling. "I should be able to take care of myself and the twins. Without help. But my life is falling apart at a time when I should be able to enjoy motherhood."

Benji pulled his chair closer to the bed and held one of her hands in his. He lightly kissed the back of it. "You don't need to do this alone. Accepting help doesn't make you weak." He squeezed her hand. "It took two people to make the twins. Stands to reason it'd take both of us to care for them."

She leveled her gaze at him. It wasn't fair. She was emotional and feeling vulnerable. His argument actually made sense.

"Don't do this out of a sense of obligation, Benji. If this isn't what you want, you can walk out of that door right now and no one else ever needs to know."

Benji slid his hand to her cheek and cradled it. His voice was soft. "Nothing in the world is more important to me than taking care of you and the twins. Are we clear on that?"

She nodded, and he leaned in and kissed her cheek. A kiss that was soft and sweet. Yet, it warmed her from the inside out.

He kissed her again, this time a closed-mouth kiss on the lips.

When he raised his eyes to hers, there was the same desire she'd seen there that night. The night they'd made the twins.

Except six months ago she'd been beautiful, and now she felt like a beached whale.

A sly smile curved the edge of his mouth and he leaned in to kiss her again.

"Should I come back later?" A male nurse hovered inside the doorway.

"No." Benji groaned, his gaze still meeting hers. "I'd liked to get her back home and settled in as soon as possible."

He moved to the sofa to give the nurse room to check Sloane's and the babies' vitals. The man put a blood pressure cuff on Sloane.

"Now's a good time to tell my mother and father they're going to be grandparents." He pulled out his cell phone.

"You're going to tell them over the phone?"

Sloane's pulse suddenly raced as she imagined Connie and Rick Bennett's reaction to the news. Rick would be mildly surprised, but Connie would be spitting fire, and she'd probably faint right on the spot. When she recovered, the woman would blame her for corrupting their son. Which she probably deserved.

And Delia. God, her friend was going to be angry with her. Delia already knew of her pregnancy. Only Sloane hadn't told her friend the whole truth about it. Like the fact that her little brother was the father.

"Why not tell them now?"

"I'm pretty sure that's the kind of conversation that should be had in person."

"We have to tell them eventually, Sloane." He kept his voice even.

"I know." Sloane frowned when the blood pressure machine beeped, and she saw the unusually high numbers. She turned to the nurse. "Can you give me a few minutes and take it again, please? I just got a little worked up. My numbers will go down in a few minutes, I promise."

The man nodded begrudgingly. "Be back in fifteen minutes."

She sighed in relief, then turned to Benji. "I know that we have to tell them, and we will. But don't you think it's better if we figure all of this out first?"

"All of what?" He sat beside her again.

"You said you're not going back to Seattle. Well, fine. But there isn't enough room in my tiny condo for me, you and all the stuff for the babies."

"So we'll sell your place and get a bigger one."

"I can't just sell my place. It needs a lot of work before I can put it on the market and…" Sloane chewed her lower lip. She didn't like talking money with Benji. Feeling as if she had her hand out.

"And?" He prodded.

"And I'm under water."

"You overpaid for the condo?"

She shook her head, her voice lowered. "I took out a second mortgage on the place." Sloane fiddled with the strap across her belly. "Don't look at me like that. I didn't spend the money on shoes or something. I took the loan out for a good reason."

"Which was?"

"I don't think that's any of your—"

"Sloane!" He inhaled deeply, then lowered his voice considerably. "Just tell me. Why did you need the money?"

"To save the farm. The crop yield hasn't been good the last few years. Plus, my grandfather needed bypass surgery last year and the insurance didn't cover everything. Do you have any idea how expensive medicine is for a cardiac patient?"

Benji stood and paced the floor. "Delia mentioned that your granddad had surgery." He turned to face her, the wheels in his head obviously turning. "Both your condo and your family's farm have second mortgages on them?"

"Yes." She whispered the word under her breath. "I had a plan. I didn't have much cash to spare, but I was paying my bills and theirs. And I was about to land the job as the creative director at the record company until..." She paused, sinking her teeth into her lower lip. She didn't want to make it seem as if she was blaming him or the twins.

"Until you couldn't work anymore because of the pregnancy." Benji slid into the seat beside her again. "I'm starting to get the picture."

They were both quiet for a moment. Then he leaned forward and gripped her hand. "Look, I know you think the worst of the folks in Magnolia Lake, but I plan to prove you wrong."

"What are you talking about?"

"Let me get the condo ready for sale."

"Even if I got top dollar for it, I'd barely break even with the second mortgage." Her grandfather had implored her not to do it, but she'd been determined to prove to him that she'd made something of herself, despite his predictions that she'd flop in "the big city." Not one of her better decisions. "Besides, if I sell my condo, where will I live?"

"You'll move to Magnolia Lake with me." His brown eyes were earnest, but his expression was neutral.

"I have no intention of moving in with my mother and grandfather." A shiver ran down her spine just thinking of it. "I'd rather live in a tent in the woods."

"Perfect. Then you'll move into the cabin with me."

A tiny ray of hope flared deep in her chest.

Benji was asking her to move into the cabin with him. Did that mean he felt something for her, too?

After their weekend together, she hadn't been able to get him out of her head. She couldn't stop wondering if a future for them was possible. But Benji was the first man she'd been with since her divorce. She cared about him too much to make him her rebound guy. Once she learned she was pregnant, she'd attributed her feelings for him to her wildly fluctuating hormones.

The same hormones that filled her body with heat as her gaze traced the sensual lines of Benji's strong physique. The same hormones that made her long for his hands to glide along her skin, the way they had when he'd made love to her.

Sloane pinched the bridge of her nose and squeezed her eyes shut, trying to shake loose the fine image of how Benji's muscles had bunched beneath his brown skin. She needed to focus on the larger implications of what he was saying.

"You're asking me to move in with you?"

"We should get married first, naturally. For the sake of the twins." He released her hand and pulled out his cell phone, tapping out a message. "But it would only be temporary."

"The marriage?" Her heart had inflated and deflated in six seconds flat.

Not that she wanted to get married again. Ever. And she still had a modicum of pride. He wanted to marry her, but only because he felt obligated to, and now he was saying it would be some kind of temporary arrangement?

He looked puzzled, then frowned with realization. "No, not the marriage. Living at the cabin would be temporary," he clarified. "I'm shooting my cousin Cole a message now. We'd live at the cabin until Cole's company can build us a permanent home."

"Hold up there, Andy Griffith." She extended her palm toward him. "I'm not agreeing to a shotgun wedding. Do people really still have those?"

"You don't want to get married?" The poor thing looked bewildered, as if he couldn't possibly imagine why a knocked-up poor girl would reject the offer to get hitched to an incredibly handsome, impossibly sexy billionaire and commence having his babies.

"Because getting married strictly because of an unexpected pregnancy worked out so well for my parents and for your sister." Baby boy bounced his generous-sized head on her bladder as if in objection.

Of course, you'd side with him. Traitor.

Sloane rubbed her belly, hoping to calm the little one.

Benji's jaw tensed. "We're not either of them."

If he said that a few more times, she'd suggest he put it on a T-shirt. But as things stood, she didn't want to aggravate him any more than she already had.

"No, we're not. They were in long-term relationships, but still couldn't make their shotgun weddings work. We had a one-night stand, Benj. A really incredible one, but still—"

"Then why not just keep doing it?" He winced and swiped a hand across his forehead. "I wasn't talking about sex…necessarily. I just meant being together. The night we spent together, it wasn't just about sex, not for me, at least."

"Not for me, either." She smiled sweetly. Or at least as sweetly as she could manage while baby boy played trampoline with her bladder and kicked underneath her ribs. "But one night of great sex and reminiscing over the past does not a marriage make. And I really do like you, Benji. Too much to watch our friendship turn into a strained, bitter relationship that'll make us and the twins miserable."

Sloane sighed, her heart twisting at the pained look on Benji's face.

He slipped his phone back in his pocket without sending the message to Cole and scrubbed a hand down his face. "You're sure about this?"

"I'm positive. Thanks for the offer, Benj, but if I ever get married again, it'll be for one reason and one reason only—that we're both head over heels in love."

Three

Benji drove Sloane's car, the silence stretching between them. She'd pretended to be upbeat, like everything would be okay, until they'd sent her to the cashier's desk once she'd been released by the doctor.

The stress and embarrassment she felt were obvious when they'd asked how she'd pay her insurance co-pay. She'd almost whispered the words, "Bill me."

When Sloane had made one last stop at the restroom, Benji had gone back to the desk and paid the entire bill. After she came back, he'd handed the receipt to Sloane and, though she'd thanked him, her face had fallen. She'd been silent ever since, staring out the passenger window the entire drive.

"Are you angry that I paid the hospital bill?" he asked finally, gripping the steering wheel tightly. The tension rolling off her shoulders was contagious.

"I appreciate what you did." She turned in his general direction as they idled at the traffic light. "I'm just angry with myself for being in a position where you felt you needed to do it."

"I wish you'd reconsider my offer."

"Thanks, but no thanks on the shotgun wedding, Benj." She adjusted her seat belt. "I know you billionaires aren't used to people telling you no. But marrying me strictly for your progeny... that's gonna be a hard pass for me."

"I was wrong." He turned into the parking lot of her condo, recalling their conversation on the dance floor. "You're stubborn as hell."

She laughed and the tension between them eased a little. He couldn't help chuckling, too.

Sloane was wrong about him. He wasn't some asshole billionaire who expected strict obedience from the people surrounding him. But when it came to business, he knew what he wanted and made it happen, whether that was developing a new app, acquiring a new company or getting the very best price when he sold his.

He applied a thumb to people's pressure points and used whatever leverage he ethically could in order to negotiate the best possible deal. It worked every time. Even with hard cases, like the Japanese company that eventually purchased his tech start-up and the block of promising companies he'd acquired.

Why couldn't he do the same with Sloane?

It wasn't a tactic he'd use on the soon-to-be mother of his children, if she'd left him any other choice. But no way would he let Sloane struggle to care for his son and daughter in a run-down condo thousands of miles away. He had no choice but to do what he did best. Apply gentle pressure to get the desired results.

When they'd stopped to get her mail, there were more envelopes stamped Final Notice. He got her and the groceries inside, settled her on the sofa and put the groceries away.

"You really don't have to do that, Benji. You're the guest, and the contractions have stopped, so I'm perfectly fine."

He shot her a look that dared her to move from the couch. For once, she didn't object. She sat back and almost seemed relieved he hadn't taken her up on her offer.

Maybe it was the same with his marriage proposal. A proposal that made perfect sense given their situations. Sloane was proud and determined. She didn't want him trying to ride in on his white horse and save the day.

He got that. Her determined attitude was one of the things he'd always admired about Sloane. So maybe what he needed to do was sweeten the pot. Make her look like the winner in the deal. Give her an offer she simply couldn't pass on.

Benji got Sloane a glass of cold water to make sure she stayed hydrated. He handed it to her and sat in a chair across the coffee table from her. He drummed his fingers on his knees, running the words through his head.

"Whatever it is you want to ask me, Benj, just say it." Sloane put the glass down on a coaster and drew her legs onto the sofa, sitting cross-legged. She rubbed her belly again.

Every time her hand drifted there, he couldn't help recalling how it'd felt when the babies moved beneath his hand. Or thinking about the fact that he was going to be a father in just a few short months.

He slid to the edge of the chair. "I'd like to make a proposal."

"Please, don't get on one knee, Benj. That'll just make it awkward for both of us. My answer hasn't changed. No shotgun wedding."

Sloane had no qualms about battering his poor ego. If he'd been afraid that the money and women chasing him would go to his head, Sloane Sutton was a sure antidote for an overinflated ego.

"I'll fix up your condo and get you top dollar for it." He cleared his throat as he studied Sloane's face. Her eyes widened with surprise, then narrowed as if she didn't like where the conversation was going. "You can keep all of the proceeds of the sale, plus I'll write you a seven-figure check, just as a way to compensate you for—"

"Having my own kids?" She was more than a little indignant as she clutched her belly protectively. "I'm not your surrogate, Benji. These are *my...*" She released a long, slow breath. "These are our twins."

"I didn't mean it that way, Sloane. It's just that I realize what a burden this has been for you trying to handle it all on your own. I just want to help."

"But let me guess, the 'price' of this help is agreeing to become Mrs. Benjamin Bennett." She gave him a pointed look, like she couldn't have possibly been more disappointed with him. Then she stood suddenly, steadying herself on the arm of the sofa before shuffling into the kitchen. "So being rich has changed you."

Her cell phone rang, and he glanced at the screen. It was the same toll-free number that had called two or three times already. Each time she'd looked at the phone and gotten agitated before sending the call to voice mail.

He sat at the kitchen island, where she was scooping ice cream into a bowl.

"Having money hasn't changed me, Sloane. I'm a businessman. It's my job to make deals and get results—in a way that's fair to both parties. That's what I'm trying to do here. Do what's best for everyone."

"You don't get to show up in my life after ten

years and assume you know what's best for me."
She snatched a bag of salt-and-vinegar potato
chips from the pantry, opened them and crumbled chips over her ice cream.

He was pretty sure a little of his lunch tried to
crawl back up his esophagus, but he made a point
not to cringe. This woman needed 24/7 supervision and a nutritional intervention.

"Okay, Sloane, maybe you're right," he said
calmly. "But I can see that you need help right
now, and I want to be there for you. Not just because of our son and daughter, but because you're
a friend. I care about you."

She looked at him, just as she stuffed an overflowing spoon of the ice-cream-and-potato-chip
concoction into her mouth. Her eyes suddenly
welled with tears and she dropped the spoon back
into the bowl.

"A year ago, I completely had my shit together."
She poked an accusing finger at him. "Then I
had to take out those loans and things were tight,
but I was managing it and, dammit, I had a plan.
And it was working. Hell, that promotion was as
good as mine." She wiped away tears angrily and

huffed, shaking her head. "I will not marry you, Benji. Especially not for money."

Pressure points.

He cared for Sloane, but what he was doing was for the good of her *and* the babies. They belonged with him back in the place they'd both known as home.

Benji leveled his gaze with hers. "You're completely opposed to us getting married, that's fine. Then just come back to Magnolia Lake with me and stay at the cabin until the twins are one year old. At the end of the year, we can have a home built in Magnolia Lake, here in Nashville or wherever you want. If you still want to walk away, no harm, no foul. But I'll still help you sell the condo. And I'll pay all of your expenses while we're living together."

Sloane looked as if she were turning the idea over in her head. She chewed on the corner of her lower lip before slowly shaking her head.

Benji came around to her side of the island and faced her. "I'll pay off the farm, too. Free and clear."

Now she paused. "Why would you do that?"

"Because I want to be with you and our children. And it'll give me a year to show you that this relationship can work for all of us."

Sloane licked her lower lip and glanced at the envelope printed with the angry red letters on the counter.

"And what if at the end of that year, I still want to walk away?"

It pained him that she'd asked, but he forced a half smile, shoved his hands in his pockets and shrugged. "Then you walk away with the seven-figure check and zero debt. Your family's farm will be paid off and you can buy a house with a yard for you and the twins. And, of course, I'm going to take care of them, regardless of what choice you make today."

Sloane nibbled on one nail as she thought. She sighed. "And you won't try to take them away from me?"

"I would never do that to you." He hadn't meant it as a dig at her and the fact that she'd chosen not to tell him about the twins. But from the way she'd lowered her gaze, she'd taken it that way.

Fine. If he had to play to the guilt she felt over what she'd done, so be it. Whatever it took to get her to yes.

"You'd pay everything off at the end of the year?"

The tension in his chest eased a bit. She was almost there. "No."

She frowned. "How much longer would I need to wait?"

"You wouldn't have to wait at all. You just say the word, and I'll make a call right now."

"Why wouldn't you wait until the end to pay them off in full?"

"Because I trust you, Sloane." He lifted her chin and gave her a faint smile. "And I don't want you to spend the rest of your pregnancy stressed about the condo or the farm."

She stepped backward, as if she needed air and space. Sloane stared at him for a moment, then pressed a hand to her stomach. "If I do this, I'm doing it for my mother and grandfather. And the twins, of course. I don't want anything for myself."

Benji swallowed hard and agreed, but deep down he hoped that it wasn't true. By the end of the year, he was determined to make her realize that they should be a family.

"One more thing…" She raked her fingers

through her curls. "If we do this, I need you to understand that this doesn't make us a couple. We're simply co-parenting the twins. I think it's best if we don't complicate things."

He nodded and forced a smile, hoping he'd managed to hide his disappointment. "Agreed. But I have a stipulation, too."

She tilted her head. "Yes?"

"Don't tell anyone about our deal."

Sloane frowned and rubbed her back. "My mother and grandfather are going to realize the truth as soon as the calls and threatening letters stop coming. It won't be hard for them to figure it out."

"Okay," Benji conceded. "But even they don't need to know that it was part of our deal. And ask them to keep everything low-key and not tell anyone where the money came from."

"And what about Delia?" Sloane frowned, her expression pained. "I don't like keeping secrets from her. These past six months…not being able to tell her the truth… It was hard." She shook her head. "I don't know if she'll ever forgive me, and the last thing I want to do is make it worse by keeping this from her."

"You didn't seem to have a problem keeping it from me."

Okay, so maybe that one was on purpose.

"All right." A deep frown still pinched her features. She nodded. "I'll move into the cabin with you until the twins' first birthday."

"Finish your ice cream." He winked. "We've got a lot to do."

"You sure she's pregnant? You know, I saw this episode of—"

"I'm positive." Benji cut his always-skeptical cousin Parker off before he could launch into another "women can't be trusted" story.

Benji adjusted the volume on the airport rental car's Bluetooth as he turned into the entrance to his parents' community in Vero Beach, Florida. He hated to leave Sloane by herself, but she'd been right. This was a conversation he needed to have in person.

"Are you sure they're yours?" Parker, known for his bluntness, sounded apologetic, which meant he was making a real effort.

"Yes." Benji's tone lacked conviction. He didn't

doubt that he was the twins' father, but he had no solid evidence to prove it.

"Okay, let's say you are the father. Do you think Sloane did this on purpose?"

"No, you know that's not Sloane's MO. I had to beg her to let me take care of her and the twins. I asked her to marry me, and she turned me down."

"You asked her to marry you?" Parker sputtered as if he was choking on whatever he'd been drinking. Knowing Park, it was probably coffee. "Are you insane?"

Benji wasn't sure how to answer that, either.

"Look, I have to go." His parents' house came into view. "See you in a week."

"Benj, it doesn't sound like you've thought this through. There are too many variables you're not accounting for. What if—"

"Goodbye, Parker." Benji ended the call and parked in the drive. He got out and put his coat on.

Delia and little Evie were spending the winter in Vero Beach, so it was the perfect time to tell his entire family. Sloane had insisted she should be there, but just talking about it had stressed her out. He'd overruled her and set out to tell his family on his own. But now that he was here, his feet felt as heavy as cement blocks as he trudged toward their front door.

"Benji? What on earth are you doing here, son? I had no idea you were in town." Rick Bennett hugged him. "Come on in. Your mother and sister will be thrilled you're here."

"That's why you didn't answer my call," his mother said, her face lighting up when she saw him. "You planned to surprise me." She hugged him tightly.

"I actually do have a surprise." He shoved his hands into his pockets when she finally released him. "Not that that's what I'd intended, it's just that it all came as a shock to me, too."

"What are you babbling about, Benji?" His sister trotted down the stairs and hugged him. "And don't wake your niece. I just put her down for a nap."

"Perfect, because I need to talk to you guys about something."

"What is it, Benji? You're scaring me." His mother frowned.

"Why don't we have a seat in the sunroom." He guided his mother to her favorite space in the house, a room filled with light that faced the pool.

"This is gonna be bad, isn't it?" His mother looked to his father for confirmation.

"Relax, Connie. Whatever Benji has to tell us, I'm sure it'll be fine." His father took a seat beside his mother on the sofa.

Delia squinted at him, her head cocked. "Oh… my… God."

"What, what is it?" His mother was in full panic mode.

"You knocked someone up, didn't you?" She was practically giddy with delight.

"How'd you know?" His face stung with heat and his heart raced.

"That's the same look I had on my face when I had to tell Mom and Dad I was pregnant with Evie. Halfway between extreme nausea and gut-wrenching terror."

That pretty much summed up how he felt. Which was ridiculous, because he was a grown man with more money than he knew what to do with. He glanced at his parents.

"So, it's true?" His mother pressed a hand to

her cheek. "We're going to be grandparents for the second time?"

Benji held his forehead. "And third."

"Wait, you're having twins, too?"

"What do you mean, *too*?" His father, who'd barely reacted to his news, turned to his sister. "You're not pregnant again, are you?"

"No, I'm not." She practically sang the words. "But a friend is."

"Benji, I didn't realize you were dating. Did you meet someone while you were in Japan?" his mother asked. Suddenly she turned toward Delia. "One of your friends is pregnant with twins? Why haven't I heard about this before?"

"I was too busy working to meet anyone while I was overseas," Benji assured his mother. "And, no, I haven't exactly been dating."

"She wasn't prepared to share it with the world because she's not with the guy," Delia responded almost simultaneously.

"So you're not in a committed relationship with this girl." His mother frowned. "What if she won't allow us to spend time with the kids? And, worse, what if she's only done this to get money from you?"

"Why does everyone in this family automatically assume that if a woman gets pregnant, it's part of some nefarious scheme?" Benji paced the floor. "Some things just *happen*."

"Benjamin Darnell Bennett." Delia folded her arms and pinned her stare on him. "Who is it that you just *happened* to knock up six months ago, before you left for Japan?"

The recognition was there in his sister's eyes, before he uttered the name. "Sloane Sutton."

His mother, father and sister all spoke at once. His mother looked like she was going to faint, his father was at least mildly interested in the entire conversation and his sister was fit to be tied.

"Benji, how could you sleep with the Sutton girl, and at your cousin's wedding?"

It wasn't like he'd taken Sloane on the dessert bar amid the miniature peach cobblers and strawberry-rhubarb pies. But he didn't think his mother would appreciate his sad attempt at humor, so he didn't respond.

"Isn't she quite a bit older than you, son?" His father almost seemed impressed.

"Half of the single women in town were after you that night. Yet the one person you chose to sleep with was my best friend?" Delia looked as if her head were about to explode. "And then you both lied to me about it."

"We didn't lie to you," Benji corrected her. "We didn't tell you, because it wasn't any of your business."

"When I asked Sloane about her babies' father, she said it was a meaningless hookup. That it had been a huge mistake. Was that a lie, too?"

His sister had hurled Sloane's words back at him, knowing that they'd pierce flesh and nick bone like a sharpened blade. He gritted his teeth.

"None of that matters now, Delia. The only thing that matters is that I'm going to be a father."

"I don't trust that girl." His mother's voice trembled. "Never did." She turned to his father. "I told you we shouldn't have had Sloane over. We should've forbidden Delia to see her."

"You're really going to blame this on me?" His father rubbed a hand over his balding head. "Besides, it seems to me that you tried that, and it didn't work."

"Why would you say that, Mom?" Benji winced. "Sloane has never given us reason to distrust her."

"Like mother, like daughter." Benji's mother

shook her head. "She barely came back to town while her grandfather was sick. Then she comes to Blake's wedding and she's all over you? I'll bet this was her plan from the start. She gets herself pregnant and she never has to work another day in her life."

"I can't believe you would say that about Sloane, that you'd even think it. She was right, you've never liked her."

"She's a better judge of character than I thought."

"Delia, Connie, I know you're both upset, but you're being much too hard on the girl. Regardless of what you might think of her mother," his father objected, "Sloane has always been smart and independent. A hard worker. Doesn't sound like the kind of woman who'd set a honey trap for some unsuspecting man. Least of all, Benji."

"That farm of theirs has been bleeding money. Now suddenly Benji comes to town rich and she's carrying his children? I don't believe it. Not until I see proof." His mother turned toward him. "We need to hire an investigator to find out exactly what Ms. Sloane has been up to since your night together. See if she's ever pulled this before. And the moment the babies are born, we're doing a paternity test."

"That isn't up to you, Mama." Benji strained to remain civil with his mother. "I'm not seeking your permission. I'm giving you an update on what's going on out of courtesy and respect."

"We appreciate that son—" his father was saying.

His mother interrupted. "But obviously, when it comes to Sloane Sutton, every ounce of the good sense you were born with flies right out the window."

"Sloane said you all would react like this. I didn't believe her, but she knows you better than I do." Benji laughed bitterly.

"Or maybe we know her better than you think you do." Delia's eyes were shiny with tears.

"What are you talking about?"

"Ask Sloane what she said would be the solution to all of her financial problems?"

His skin vibrated with anger. His jaw clenched so tightly it ached. "Why don't you tell me, since you seem so eager to?"

"About a year ago, she and I were joking that a couple of rich husbands would be the solution to all of our problems." Delia swiped at the corner of her eye. "I guess she wasn't joking, after all."

"Stop it. Both of you." Benji looked from his mother to his sister. "Whether you like it or not, Sloane Sutton will be the mother of my son and daughter. And I've invited her to move into the cabin at the lake with me."

Delia and his mother started talking at once.

"I don't want to hear any more about this. I'm *not* investigating her, I don't need a paternity test and she *is* moving into the cabin with me. So, if you'd like to meet your grandchildren and your niece and nephew, I suggest you find a way to treat her with respect, beginning with an apology."

Benji turned to Delia. "Maybe Sloane didn't handle this the way she should've, but I believe she did it for what she thought were the right reasons. She's your best friend, Delia, and she's always had your back. Too bad she can't say the same of you."

He left, slamming the front door behind him.

Four

"Thank you again, Benji." Sloane shifted in her seat, adjusting the seat belt as they made the drive from Nashville to Magnolia Lake. She was grateful, of course, for everything Benji had done for her and her family.

As promised, he'd gotten on the phone right away, contacted his accountant and made arrangements to pay off both properties immediately. Then he'd gotten on the phone with his cousin Cole Abbott to see if he could either send a small crew to Nashville to work on Sloane's condo renovation or recommend a local crew.

That night, he'd helped her pack her luggage

and hired movers to pack up the rest of the space and put her furniture in storage.

Within forty-eight hours, a crew had started renovating her condo. Benji had put her up at a hotel while he flew to Vero Beach to see his parents.

Sloane was grateful. How could she not be? But there was also a part of her that hated that she'd allowed Benji to do any of that for her. That she hadn't been in a position to do it herself.

The older women back in Magnolia Lake had called her independent, as if it were a bad thing. She carried that designation like a mantle of honor. She was glad they thought of her that way. The very opposite of how she'd always viewed her own mother.

Abigail Sutton had been dependent upon one man or another her entire life. Sloane's father. A succession of live-in boyfriends. Sloane's grandfather.

Sloane had vowed that she would never be like her mother. Though she loved her, she'd found it hard to respect her once she'd become a teenager and truly understood her mother's relationships with her boyfriends. She'd accepted their poor treatment as long as they'd paid the bills.

Sloane would never be that woman, yet the arrangement she had with Benji made her feel that she was teetering dangerously close to becoming just like her.

"I was happy to do it, Sloane." Benji's response brought her back to the moment. His words were kind, but he'd been in a foul mood since he'd returned from Florida. He refused to talk about what had happened with his parents, other than to say things had gone badly.

He'd advised her not to bother calling Delia. But Delia had been her best friend since they were ten. She was her only close friend. So she'd tried calling anyway. Each call had gone straight to voice mail.

Her friend hated her, Benji was at odds with his family and all of it was her fault.

"I know you said you don't want to talk about how things went at your parents' house—"

"Still don't." His jaw tensed, and he gripped the wheel tighter.

She had the overwhelming desire to hold him and whisper in his ear that everything would be all right. But aside from the constraints of the car he'd rented, there was the reality that they weren't in a relationship and didn't share that kind of emotional intimacy.

It was just as well.

In her experience, that kind of intimacy made one incredibly vulnerable. She'd been ass up in stirrups at least once a month since she'd learned she was pregnant. That was more than enough vulnerability for a lifetime.

"Let's talk about baby names instead." A smile curved the edge of his mouth, the first she'd seen since he'd returned from Vero Beach. "We need a boy's name and a girl's name. Got any prospects?"

She shrugged. "Not really."

He furrowed his brow. "I'm no pregnancy expert, but I thought that dreaming up baby names was one of the things moms-to-be spent their time doing."

"No one has ever accused me of being typical." She laughed bitterly. "And I didn't say I hadn't given their names any thought. It'd be nice to call them something other than Little Dude and Buttercup. What I said is that I don't have any prospects, as in I haven't settled on anything."

The one male name that Sloane felt strongly about was Benjamin. But back when she'd intended to keep Benji's paternity a secret, there was no way she could've risked naming the baby after his father without creating speculation. Now that their families and the entire town of Magnolia Lake would know, there was no reason Little Dude couldn't be a junior.

"What names have you considered?"

She was quiet for a moment. "For her? Scarlett."

"As in O'Hara?"

"As in Johansson."

Benji nodded thoughtfully. "I do like a woman who can play a badass Marvel superhero. What else you got?"

"Vivian."

"As in Leigh?"

"No, as in Julia Roberts' character in *Pretty Woman*." Sloane grinned. "Do we need to talk about your obsession with *Gone with the Wind*?"

"It's my mom's favorite movie." Benji shrugged, frowning at the mention of his mother. "And do

I need to spell out the reasons I'm diametrically opposed to naming my daughter after a character that was a prostitute?"

"Hey, sex workers are people, too." Sloane poked his bicep. "But point taken. What about Bailey?"

"I love the name Bailey for a girl." He nodded. "Let's stick a pin in that one. And for Little Dude?" He gave her a sarcastic grin.

"Phillip, Beau or maybe Benjamin." Sloane looked straight ahead, but her cheeks warmed as Benji looked over at her briefly before returning his eyes to the road.

"I'm honored that you'd propose making him a junior. But I've never liked the idea of putting additional pressure on a boy to be like his father. I want our kids to do or be anything they want. And I'm grateful they'll have the resources to do that."

"Me, too." She glanced over at him, realizing for the first time how grateful she was that her children would never struggle like she and her mother did.

He squeezed her hand and gave her a warm smile before putting his hand back on the wheel and changing lanes. "I like Beau. It goes nicely with Bailey, don't you think?"

"Beau and Bailey." She repeated the names softly. "What do you think, Little Dude and Buttercup? Do you think you can deal with Beau and Bailey? Think carefully before you answer. You're going to have those names your entire lives. Unless you become actors or strippers." When Benji's eyes widened, she laughed. "Relax, I'm kidding."

He sighed, shaking his head. "If your way of cheering me up is supposing that our daughter might become a stripper, I'm gonna need you to work on your cheering-up game."

"Who said I was talking about her? I could've been referring to him. Just think, our son could grow up to be the next Magic Mike."

"If you weren't carrying Beau and Bailey, I'd put you out on the side of the highway and make you walk the rest of the way to Magnolia Lake." He laughed.

Both the babies moved.

"They just responded to the sound of your voice," she told Benji, then spoke again, projecting her voice down toward her belly as she placed her hands on either side of it. "Does that mean you two like your names?" When there was no movement, she told Benji, "Say their names again."

"Beau and Bailey, this is your father. You two okay in there?"

Beau seemed to stretch his legs and Bailey responded by doing the same.

"I think we have a winner." Sloane rubbed her hand in a circle over the babies, her heart full and her eyes stinging with tears. "Beau and Bailey, it is. Though I think it should be something like Beaumont. Beau should just be his nickname."

"I like it." Benji nodded, his handsome face animated with a genuine smile. "And since their first names begin with the same letter as mine, we should pick middle names that begin with the letter S."

"I like that idea." Sloane smiled. "God, please tell me that co-parenting will be this easy for the entire eighteen years."

Benji looked uneasy. He shifted the conversation to a different topic. "So about the twins' room. I thought, while we're at the cabin, that they could share a room. That would make middle-of-the-night feedings and diaper changes easier. That'd also leave one guest room and a room for the nanny."

"A nanny?" Sloane laughed. "I'm not really the nanny type, Daddy Warbucks. Besides, I'm not working right now, so I can handle it."

"I'm renting some space and setting up a satellite office in town, but I'll try to be there as much as I can in the beginning. Still, I think you're underestimating how challenging it is to take care of one baby, let alone two."

"Delia managed with Evie."

"She only had one baby to deal with." The corners of his mouth tugged down at the mention of his sister. "And my mother lived with Delia and her new husband for the first two months to help out. If you ask me, she helped them right out of their marriage."

Sloane refrained from agreeing with Benji, though there was some truth to what he'd said. "Their relationship was never on solid ground because they got married for the wrong reason."

Delia and Frank's marriage had been strained and volatile from the start. He'd resented her family for pressuring him to marry Delia once she got pregnant. She'd been angry because their life together wasn't the domestic fantasy she'd been dreaming of her entire life.

"True." And just like that, Benji was back to growling one-word answers.

"If you don't want to talk about what happened down in Florida for me, then do it for Little…for Beau and Bailey. This silence and the suspense are completely stressing me out. Which means it's stressing the twins out, too."

Benji sighed heavily. "Okay, since you're determined to talk about it…you were right. My mother didn't take the news well. In fact, she questions whether the twins are mine."

"She thinks I'm lying?" Sloane's chest tightened. She knew Connie Bennett wasn't her biggest fan, but even she hadn't seen that coming. "How could she believe I'd do something so horrible?"

"I don't know." He shrugged. "But, at the very least, she questions your motives. She's overreacting, I know, but what my sister said only confirmed her suspicions."

Her heart squeezed in her chest. Connie not being thrilled that she was the mother of Benji's twins wasn't a surprise. And though she knew Delia would be upset that she hadn't told her the truth right away, she certainly wouldn't have imagined that her best friend would turn on her and give her mother more ammunition.

"What did Delia say?" The sound of her own heart thumping filled her ears.

"Did you say that finding a rich husband would be the key to solving your financial worries?"

Sloane nearly denied it, but the memory of their conversation over drinks that night came back to her.

"I was joking. We both were. Delia knows that."

Benji's expression was stoic. "Now she thinks maybe you weren't kidding."

It hurt that her best friend could think for even a moment that she'd purposely done this. That she'd used her brother and would use her own children for financial gain.

"And what do you think, Benji?" Sloane asked softly, studying his profile as he focused on the road that stretched ahead of them.

"I told them that didn't sound anything like the independent woman I've always known. And that if they hoped to ever meet the twins, they needed to apologize for how poorly they'd treated their mother."

Her heart soared momentarily. He'd defended her to his mother and sister, had taken her side over theirs. Then her heart crashed nearly as quickly, as she realized she'd driven a wedge between Benji, his mother and sister.

The thing she'd always admired about the Bennetts was how close they were. Nothing had been able to come between them. Nothing except for her.

The guilt lay in her gut like a rock, beside the two precious babies she was carrying.

"Thank you for believing me, Benj. I really appreciate you standing up for me. But I don't want to be the cause of contention between you and your family."

"That was their choice," he said abruptly, frowning. "And they can choose to apologize whenever they're ready." He heaved a sigh. "Enough about that. Let's talk about something else."

"Like what?"

"Like what it feels like to be growing not one but two human beings inside you."

Her mouth stretched in an involuntary smile.

"It's incredible." She massaged her tummy, prompting movement from Beau. "I never really aspired to be a mother. Not even during my marriage. That's one of the reasons it ended."

"Why didn't you want children?" His tone was tentative. As if, he wasn't sure he wanted to know the answer.

"It's hard to get that corner office when you have to take off for maternity leave and OB appointments. Sucks, but it's true." The record company hadn't been overt about it, but there was a reason most of the women who worked there were young and unattached. "Besides, I didn't think I had it in me to be self-sacrificing and I'm the last person on earth who should be dishing out life advice."

"What made you change your mind?"

"Because from the moment I've known about them, they're all I think about. I even dream about them. I know I won't be a perfect mom by any stretch of the imagination. But I'll try my hardest, because that's what they deserve."

She wiped away the tears that leaked from her eyes.

"You will be, Sloane." Benji's voice was as

soothing as a warm hug, the kind her grand-mother used to give her as a little girl.

"I just hope they appreciate the fact that I've sacrificed my four-cups-of-coffee-a-day habit and my long, hot soaks in the bathtub." She spoke to her belly again. "If you're considering how to reward Mommy, how about sleeping through the night by two months. I'd really appreciate that."

Benji and Sloane laughed.

"I get why you had to give up the coffee. But why'd you have to give up baths?"

"It's not that I can't take them at all. It's just that the water shouldn't be too hot, and I'm not supposed to soak for too long. More practically, there's the concern that once I'm in the tub, I won't be able to get out. The hazards of living alone." She forced a laugh.

He squeezed her hand and smiled. "Thankfully, living alone won't be an issue anymore."

Dammit. The waterworks were starting again.

Benji got Sloane settled in at the cabin and went out to stock the place with groceries. He'd asked Sloane if she wanted to come along, but she wasn't quite ready to make her Magnolia Lake pregnancy debut. He understood, and, to be honest, he was grateful for a little time alone to process what had happened over the past few days.

He was a doer. He saw what needed to be done and he made it happen. Those were the moments when he felt most in control. Even before he'd signed the multibillion-dollar deal for his company, he'd been the kind of take-control guy who knew how to get shit done, despite whatever obstacle was thrown in his way. He loved it when a competitor or investor dismissed him, insisting that what he wanted to do was impossible. He thrived on the challenge of making doubters eat their words.

But that was business. What was happening between him and Sloane was deeply personal.

His instincts and emotions were magnified because it was Sloane Sutton—his longtime crush. Seeing her again for the first time in nearly a decade, dancing with her, kissing her, making love to her... All of it had created feelings exponentially more powerful than anything he'd experienced.

It had hurt like hell when Sloane had rejected his offer to travel to Japan with him.

So when Parker, his mother and his sister had attacked Sloane, he'd taken it more personally than he would've if the attack had been directed at him.

He'd defended her, and he'd meant every word. He believed in Sloane, believed that she'd never do the things his family was accusing her of.

But when all was quiet, small doubts crept in, making him wonder if he hadn't been as charming or as lucky as he imagined himself to be. Had Sloane's dire financial situation been a factor in her decision to spend the night with him? If so, maybe their birth-control failure wasn't an accident at all.

He massaged his throbbing forehead and dismissed the ugly thoughts.

"Benji, I didn't realize you were back in town." Nanette Henderson, owner of the Magnolia Lake General Store, approached him with a wide smile. "How long you in town for?"

She and her husband, Ralph, had owned the town's general store for as long as he could remember.

Benji leaned down to give the kindly woman a big hug. "I'm moving back home. Not to the old house, but out to my cabin. Until I can get something built in town."

"That's fantastic news! It'll be good to have you back around here." She grinned. "You have to come out to the house and have lunch with me and Ralph one afternoon. I'll show you the scrapbook I'm keeping of all the magazines you've been in."

This was the kind of thing he missed about being home. People who were genuinely happy for you when you succeeded. Who didn't see you as a threat. He just hoped that Sloane would feel the same about returning to their roots and giving Beau and Bailey a life here.

"Yes, ma'am, that sounds nice. Only I didn't know you read business and tech magazines." He grabbed a shopping cart.

"Can't reveal all my secrets." She chuckled softly. "I might be an old bird, but that doesn't mean I can't learn a few new tricks." She winked at him. "Just let me know if you need anything."

The woman walked away to greet another customer in the store.

Benji grabbed everything they might possibly need, including a few items he'd seen in Sloane's bathroom at the condo: shampoo, conditioner, bodywash and lotion.

When he rolled his cart down the baby aisle, he got lost reviewing the endless formulas, baby food, diapers, bottles and pacifiers.

It'd be a while before they needed those things. Still, it wouldn't hurt to be prepared with a few essentials. He grabbed two packs of newborn diapers and some bottles with nipples that the package claimed were ideal for newborns. Then his eye was drawn to another item. He smiled and dropped it in the cart.

It was strange to be in the cabin alone while Benji was in town. This would be her home for the next year and three months. Benji had told her to make herself at home, but it still felt like she was intruding.

He'd given Sloane her choice of bedrooms and she'd selected one of the larger guest bedrooms that had lots of light and an unobstructed view of the lake. It was next door to the bedroom they agreed their infant twins would share.

"Beau and Bailey." She said their names again as she stood by the window, staring out onto the lake. Was it silly that she already missed calling them Little Dude and Buttercup?

The sound of tires on the gravel drive and the slam of a door indicated that Benji had arrived with the groceries. She put on her coat and shoes and went outside to help.

"You'll catch a cold. Besides, I distinctly remember Dr. Carroll telling you not to lug around groceries."

"I'll take the light ones." Hopefully, there was a bag of salt-and-vinegar potato chips in there somewhere.

"No." Benji's answer was firm and his stare indicated he didn't intend to address the subject again. "If you want to help, stay inside and start putting the refrigerated goods away."

"Fine," she muttered under her breath and went inside, where the warmth of the wood-burning fireplace greeted her. "You can't blame a girl for trying to help."

"Do you want to end up on full bed rest?" His patience was wearing thin.

"God, no."

"Then cooperate or I'll be on the phone with Dr. Carroll before you know it."

"I've decided to switch to a doctor who's closer. So, sadly, she won't be my doctor anymore."

"I'll tell the new guy." He carried in an armload of groceries and set them on the counter. "No reaching high into the cabinets, either." In response to her eye roll, he added, "Don't make me take you over my knee."

"Sounds fun." She emptied the contents of one of the bags onto the counter.

His eyes darkened, and he bit his lower lip. "You're intentionally trying to drive me mad, aren't you?" He turned and headed back outside.

"Maybe," she whispered under her breath.

"I heard that." He held up a finger on his way out the door.

Sloane laughed. Living with Benji might not be so bad, after all.

Sloane wiped down the counter and turned on the dishwasher. She'd sliced her thumb while cutting onions with the super sharp, chef-worthy knives, but she and Benji had survived her first attempt at cooking dinner, so she counted the meal as a success.

It wasn't that she was incapable of cooking.

After all, she could read a cookbook as well as the next person. But her execution was lacking due to limited practice. Before she'd found herself out of a job, she'd had very little time for cooking. Her job kept her busy. Most days she just stopped at one greasy spoon or another late at night when she was dragging her tired behind home.

Once she was pregnant, she'd spent the majority of those months at home subsisting on the limited foods that she managed to keep down, due to the acute morning sickness that lasted throughout the day and most nights. She hadn't been in any hurry to cook a fancy meal.

But tonight was the first night she and Benji spent in what would be their home together for the next fifteen months. It seemed like a good time to make the effort.

Now she was exhausted. She just wanted to take a hot shower and hit the bed. She turned off the kitchen light and headed toward her room. Sloane knocked on the open door of the master bedroom.

"Hey, Benj. I just wanted to say good-night," she called, not seeing him. The scent of lavender and bergamot filled the room, but she didn't see a candle burning.

Benji stepped out of the bedroom, his shirt-sleeves pushed up to his elbows. He was drying his hands on a towel.

"Actually, I have a surprise for you. Come here." He reached his hand out to her and she took it, following him inside the master bath-room.

The most divine scent rose from the tub filled with water.

"You said you missed taking a bath and I saw this bath bomb in the grocery store, specifically for pregnant women. It's designed to help you relax. I would've done it in your room, but this is the only tub in the cabin."

"Thank you, Benji. This was sweet of you."

His sheepish smile deepened. "I made sure the temperature isn't too hot. Just don't stay in the water more than forty-five minutes and every-thing should be fine. I'll help you in and when you're ready to get out you can holler. And I'll keep my eyes closed, I promise."

"You've seen the entire package up close and personal, so I don't think we have to worry about that." She smiled. "Not to mention how much of me you'll be seeing when I go into labor. That is, if you'd like to be in the room with me when they're born."

"I wouldn't miss being there for anything in the world." He smiled faintly.

"Good." Sloane hadn't realized until now how much she wanted Benji to be there. "I need to grab a few things from my room first, but then I'll be back."

Benji waved his hand at a stash of items beside the tub. The bottles were too full to be hers, but they were the hair- and body-product brands that she used.

"You don't miss anything, do you?"

"Not when it comes to the people and things that are important to me." His gaze held hers.

Sloane was sure her heart skipped a beat. Her body, already filled with heat, reacted to him. His sweet words. His thoughtful actions. And to the memory of when she'd last stood in this bathroom, his hungry gaze sweeping over her.

She wanted him—more now than she had then.

But she was full of hormones going wild so her judgment was not to be trusted. It wouldn't be fair to toy with his feelings, knowing that when the fog cleared they might both feel very differently.

She excused herself to grab her pajamas and robe, needing to escape the magnetic power of those penetrating brown eyes.

Benji reviewed his email at his bedroom desk. A college basketball game played in the background with the sound turned down low. Even after his assistant screened his emails, he had countless requests for consulting gigs, business proposals and messages from potential investors who wanted to get in on the ground floor of whatever project he planned to take on next.

His parents had thought he'd settle down and retire at the ripe old age of twenty-five. Travel the world and perfect his golf swing. But the truth was, he'd be lost without his work. Not because his work defined him, but because he loved what he did. Playing with data, creating programs that would solve problems. He'd never even considered slowing down, let alone retiring. But seeing Sloane again had changed everything.

Since their encounter six months earlier, he

hadn't been able to get their night together out of his head. Nor had he been able to dismiss the idea of picking up where they'd left off that night at the cabin. But now he was even more enamored with her.

He was only twenty-five and at the height of his career. Being a father and settling down to raise a family were the last things on his mind. Yet, when he'd seen Sloane's belly, round and full, her skin glowing, an unfamiliar feeling had gripped his chest. He was overcome with the need to take care of and protect her and their babies. Even if he was forced to do so on her terms.

Maybe he'd been impetuous to suggest marriage, but he was on the clock. Because at the end of their agreed-upon fifteen months together, he was determined to make Sloane see that he truly cared for her and that they should raise the twins together.

"Benj, would you do me a favor?" Sloane called from the bathroom.

"Anything. What is it?" He approached the open door tentatively, sensitive to respecting her privacy.

Sloane sat with her hands and arms covering

her breasts and her knees drawn up. She handed him her soapy bath sponge. "Would you mind washing my back? I can't reach that part in the middle and it's been dry and itchy all day."

"Sure." He pushed his sleeves up farther and leaned over her, scrubbing her back. It produced so many suds that he hated to waste them. He scrubbed her arms, then her legs and her feet.

"Thanks. I think it's time for me to get out now."

"Right." He grabbed a towel and held it up for her, averting his eyes as she stood and wrapped it around herself. He helped her out of the tub.

"Thank you. You don't think about things like taking a bath or how difficult it is to dry your legs and feet when you can't even see them."

"Let me." He grabbed another towel and dried her lower legs and feet, painfully aware of how close he was to the space between her thighs. The memory of her warmth and taste washed over him, making his movements stilted and un-coordinated.

Regardless of all the things he'd accomplished in his life, there was something about Sloane Sutton that still reduced him to a bumbling, inexperienced teenager.

"All done." When he stood, she gazed up at him with the same heat in her eyes he'd seen that night. She licked her lower lip and his shaft instantly hardened.

He honestly hadn't drawn her a bath as a prelude to taking her to bed. He'd done it because it was something she missed. And after their long drive from Nashville and the delicious meal she'd made for them, it was his way of showing his appreciation.

But he couldn't tear his gaze away from her lips. Couldn't stop wanting her.

With one hand, she still clutched the towel around her. With the other, she grabbed his shirt and pulled him closer as she lifted onto her toes.

He leaned down and claimed her mouth with a hungry, raw kiss, his tongue gliding along hers.

His arms slipped around her waist, though he was careful of her belly, which was pressed against him.

Sloane let the towel slip to the floor, and his hands glided along her silky, smooth skin. He caressed the curve at the small of her back, gripped her firm bottom.

He'd appreciated the undulating curves of her fit body six months ago. But now her curves were fuller—her belly firm and round, her hips and bottom wider than they were before. And her full breasts with their darkened peaks and larger areolae were the most sensual things he'd ever seen.

The remarkable changes to her body made her sexier. Every one of those changes, and the babies growing inside her, had stemmed from the seed he'd planted six months before.

Nothing he'd ever done had made him feel more powerful than this. Knowing he'd started life inside her.

She tugged his shirt free from his pants, and her hands roamed his bare chest. Her thumb flicked his nipple, making him painfully hard.

He groaned against her mouth.

"I want you." Her warm breath skittered against his skin.

"You know I want you, Sloane, but you're hormonal." He'd spent the plane ride between Florida and Nashville reading about what to expect during pregnancy. "I don't want to do anything you'll regret in the morning."

Her eyes twinkled, and one edge of her mouth turned up in a naughty smile that did wicked things to his body.

"I promise you, I won't regret it." She broke away from him and headed toward the bedroom, calling over her shoulder. "And neither will you."

The last vestige of his control snapped when she turned and strode into his bedroom wearing nothing but the ink on her brown skin. She sat on the edge of his bed, one leg crossed over the other.

"I'm the only one naked. There's something very wrong with this picture." Her dark eyes flashed.

He couldn't disagree.

Benji stripped out of his clothing, titillated by Sloane's obvious admiration as she watched him.

He stepped forward, following her as she scooted up the bed and lay on her back, drinking in his hungry gaze.

Benji kissed Sloane before trailing kisses down her neck and chest. He worshipped the hard, fat brown peaks, laving them with his tongue as she writhed beneath him. He palmed the heavy globes, sucking on her beaded tips until she moaned with pleasure.

He kissed his way down her body and over her belly. There was honestly nothing sexier than Sloane Sutton in all her pregnant glory.

Benji kissed her mound, shielded by a patch of dark curls. He tasted her, reveling in her scent and her escalating whimpers as he teased her with his tongue.

She rested her hands on either side of his head and moved against his mouth. He gripped her thighs, opening her wide as he varied the speed, pressure and placement of his tongue. Sloane's body tensed, then she cried out his name. Her body trembled and her core pulsed.

The sight was enough to make a weaker man come undone.

He climbed up beside Sloane and held her with her back pressed against his chest. Benji buried his nose in her damp hair, losing himself in the warmth and fragrance of her soft skin. He inhaled the notes of lavender, bergamot and frankincense.

"You've always been beautiful, Sloane, but

never more than you are right now." He kissed her ear, resting one hand above her belly and the other below it on the other side.

"Funny, because I feel like a double-wide trailer." She laughed, placing her hands over his. "But I do appreciate your willingness to pretend otherwise."

"I've never lied to you, Sloane. So trust me when I tell you that your body is amazing."

She turned to face him. "Really?"

"Really." He kissed her.

"Good." She climbed on top of him, planting her hands on his chest. "Because I need to feel you inside me, Benji."

His palm rested on the tattoo on her hip as she guided him to her entrance. Her eyes fluttered, and her breath hitched as she sank down, taking him deeper.

The sensation of being buried in her wet heat sent waves of electricity up his spine. They moved together, their pace building, until they'd both found their release.

He held her in his arms, hoping this was the first step to convincing her to stay.

Five

Benji rolled over and threw one arm across his face to shield it from the sunlight creeping in through the window. It had been a month since Sloane had moved in. He loved sharing his home with her and having her in his bed at night. But each night, after he'd fallen asleep, Sloane returned to her own bed. No matter how many times he'd invited her to stay.

There was a knock at his bedroom door. "Benj, can I come in?"

It was a funny question, when he'd never wanted her to leave his bed in the first place.

"Yeah," he grumbled. He turned onto his stomach and calculated how many more minutes of sleep he could squeeze in before his 9:00 a.m. business call. "Come in."

She practically waddled into the room, her full stomach visible before he caught a glimpse of her lovely face. Her odd expression alarmed him.

He sat up quickly, wiping the sleep from his eyes. "Is everything okay?"

"I'm fine." She pressed a hand to her forehead. "But there's a guy here who claims to be trying out for a chef position."

"Shit." Benji looked at his watch. He'd forgotten that he'd set up an appointment with a personal chef. He was supposed to be cooking them breakfast right now. "His name is Marcellus. Can you show him in and tell him to get started?"

A loud clang came from the kitchen.

"Sounds like he's already setting up." Her tone and expression registered annoyance.

"Something wrong?"

"No, of course not." The twist of her mouth contradicted her words.

"Remember our deal. You be straight with me, and I promise to do the same." Benji patted the bed beside him and stretched while she tried to find a position that was comfortable. "So what's with the face? You don't like Marcellus?"

"I don't have any reason not to like him. I don't know him. Which is why it's kind of weird to have him in my...our kitchen, cooking my breakfast."

He chuckled. "You don't share the same opinion about Caitlin coming in twice a week to tidy up and do the laundry."

"True," she conceded. "But having someone else clean the bathrooms and fold the laundry doesn't feel like an assault on my domestic skills."

"You're insulted that I hired Marcellus? I thought you'd be thrilled."

"Tell me the truth. Is my cooking that bad? I mean, I know I probably lean a little too heavily on the chicken surprise casserole, but it's good, isn't it?"

"It's delicious, babe. It's just not much of a surprise anymore." He chuckled, pulling her into his arms and kissing her cheek. "I just thought it was important that we add some variety to our diet. Make sure that you and the twins are getting some balanced nutrition."

"You're right. I've got a dozen cookbooks. I can find something else to cook."

"I've watched you in the kitchen cooking. You get tired and your back hurts from standing." He rubbed her back, and she practically cooed with pleasure and melted against him. He kissed her ear, then her jaw. "Let me do this for you." He added with a big smile, "For us."

"Ha, ha, ha." She punched him in the gut. "Fine. I'll eat Marcellus's cooking. But I don't have to like it."

"Fair enough. And if you don't, we'll send him packing. But give him a fair chance. Say…two weeks?"

"Okay." She shuffled toward the door.

"Where are you going?" He caught her hand in his, hoping to talk her into sleeping in with him for a few more minutes.

"If we're having company for breakfast, I'd like to look a little less like a disaster." She indicated the peanut-butter-and-jelly stain on her robe.

"Speaking of company… Blake and Savannah have been trying to get us to come to dinner for the past two weeks. Savannah's starting to think you don't like her."

"I don't dislike her. I just don't know that I'm ready to be paraded through town like the resident harlot."

"You're not being fair, Sloane. Give them a chance. I don't think folks here are nearly as judgmental as you believe."

"I'll consider it." Sloane shrugged. "Have you decided when we'll get started on the twins' room?"

Home improvement wasn't his gift. And what was the point of being a billionaire if you still had to do all of the tasks you hated yourself? But Sloane didn't see it that way. She wanted the twins' room to be special and bear their personal touch.

"Which reminds me…" He reached into the bedside stand and dug out his wallet. "There's a new interior decorator in town. She's looking to build her portfolio and she has some really great ideas for the twins' room." He handed her a business card.

Sloane's expression sank as she studied the card. "I know you don't think I can paint the room myself, which I totally could, by the way."

"What part of 'no strenuous activity' are you not getting, Sloane Sutton?"

"You didn't seem to mind last night when I was on top."

Her defiant gaze made him want to both spank her and toss her onto the bed and make love to her. Right now, he wasn't sure which feeling was more dominant.

Benji climbed out of bed, determined to keep his cool. "You're not painting the room and I suck at stuff like that. Cole is sending over one of his guys as soon as he can."

"I know this won't be your permanent home, but the twins will be in that room for at least a year. It's where they'll begin their lives. I want it to be special."

"Of course you do, and it will be, I promise." He picked up his phone and opened his calendar. His schedule was clear for the afternoon. "Tell you what. Why don't we do some shopping for Beau and Bailey this afternoon? We'll drive into Gatlinburg and go to the mall. When we get back, Marcellus will have dinner ready."

"Okay." She didn't look nearly as thrilled about

the prospect as he'd hoped, but at least she wasn't talking about painting anymore.

Sloane sat on the floor in the middle of what would eventually become the twins' room. She looked around at the shiplap walls and the window that overlooked a pretty wooded area.

Benji had the movers remove the guest bed and store it in a shed out back. The twins' cribs, still in their boxes, rested against the wall. Sloane put more of the adorable little graphic onesies on hangers and hung them in the closet. All of the clothing on the left side of the closet was for Bailey, all of the clothing on the right for Beau. A growing stash of baby toys, furniture and other items lined the floor of the closet. Pairs of little shoes were on the shelf above.

Sloane sat in the chair in the center of the closet. Benji had insisted she keep it there after she made the mistake of sitting on the carpeted floor, sorting clothes, and then required his help to get up.

She'd been living with Benji in the cabin for the past six weeks. They'd eaten breakfast and dinner together every day, and thanks to Marcellus's mouthwatering culinary skills, she didn't have to cook or do the dishes. Sloane didn't have to do any major cleaning, thanks to Caitlin. And she'd had time to binge-watch all of the shows she'd missed when she was working crazy hours for the past few years. She should be a completely content lady of leisure.

Then why was she bored out of her mind?

The babies would be here soon enough, and they'd keep her busy. Her mother had reminded her often enough how "lucky" she was to be with a man who "was swimming in cash" *and* adored her and their unborn babies. As if she'd hit the lotto.

But she wasn't "with" Benji. True, they lived together temporarily. And they'd slept together frequently. But she'd always returned to her own bed. They weren't a couple, and this wasn't a fairy tale. When the calendar turned on the twins' first birthday, they would go their separate ways.

She wasn't like her mother. She wouldn't rely on one man or another to take care of her and the twins. Sloane had made it on her own just fine before. Once she could find another job, she'd do it again.

A tightness gripped her and she gasped. She rubbed her hand in a circle on her abdomen.

The discomfort was unlike anything she'd felt before.

"No need to be alarmed." She whispered the words under her breath.

It was probably just more Braxton Hicks contractions. She hadn't felt them in a while. Not since Benji had appointed himself her personal water and nutrition dictator. Still, she glanced at her fitness watch. She needed to make note of the time, just in case it happened again.

She got up and moved back into the twins' room, opened a box of diapers and began stacking them in the pretty changing table they'd purchased the week before.

The walls still hadn't been painted, nor had the cribs been assembled. But the room was slowly beginning to take shape. Besides, they still had more than a month to get everything done.

Another bout of pain racked her, taking her breath and nearly making her drop to her knees. She stumbled forward, her weight on the changing station as she gathered herself. She looked at her watch. It'd been a little over ten minutes since the last one. Her new OB, Dr. Miller, had advised her to call him if she had four or more contractions in an hour—a possible indication of preterm labor, which could be dangerous for her and the babies. If the contractions continued at this rate, she'd call Dr. Miller, just to be safe.

She inhaled deeply, her eyes drifting closed, and slowly released her breath. As she did, she tried hard to let go of the tension and stress that built in her chest.

Sloane put aside the diapers she'd been stacking and went to the kitchen to get a glass of water. She poured the glass and downed it, quickly pouring another for herself. She checked her watch. Just a few more seconds and she'd know whether the contractions were coming at a consistent clip.

She howled, dropping the glass, which crashed to the floor and shattered. Her eyes watered from the intensity of the contraction.

Sloane drew in a long, slow breath through her nose and released it.

Benji had flown to New York for a meeting and was scheduled to be back later in the day. He'd suggested that her mother stay with her during his three-day trip. Or that she stay at Blake and Savannah's house in his absence. But she'd grown tired of being fussed over and treated like she was incapable of doing anything for herself.

It was just three days and she wasn't expected to deliver for another six weeks, at around thirty-eight weeks. Only, she was beginning to wonder if the twins had gotten the memo.

Sloane held her belly as she moved to the sofa, thankful for the private, in-home childbirth coaching Benji had insisted that they go through.

Breathe in. Breathe out. Breathe in. Breathe out.

No need to call the doctor and alarm everyone until she was sure there was just cause.

She closed her eyes, lay back on the sofa and kept breathing, wishing that Benji was there to hold her hand and assure her everything would be all right.

But as the pain moved through her, something felt very wrong.

Benji sprinted through the tiny local airport to his waiting car as fast as his legs would carry him. Marcellus had called to tell him that Sloane was experiencing preterm labor and he was taking her to the hospital.

He should never have left her alone, regardless of what she said. It was his job to protect her and the twins, and he was failing. He only hoped that his failure hadn't put Sloane or the twins in jeopardy.

He shouldn't have taken no for an answer. He should've either insisted that her mother come and stay with her or packed her up and carted her to Blake and Savannah's place, even if he'd had to carry her, kicking and screaming.

It was a mistake he wouldn't make again.

The rubber on his tires peeled as he took off for the hospital.

Sloane's skin was flushed, and it felt like it was one hundred degrees in her hospital room, thanks to the magnesium sulfate being pumped into her veins via the IV stuck in her arm.

She was little more than thirty-two weeks. Her doctor was determined to hold off delivery as long as safely possible, to give the twins more time to develop. Which was why she was also being given steroids to help develop their little lungs, in the event that the magnesium couldn't slow the preterm labor enough.

She was agitated and cranky. Most of all she was terrified. More for the babies than for herself. If something happened to either of them, she'd never forgive herself. Benji wouldn't forgive her, either.

How many times had he reminded her to keep her cell phone charged? And hadn't he insisted that she shouldn't be alone? She hadn't listened. She'd thought Benji was overreacting. Being melodramatic. But he'd been right all along.

Thank goodness Marcellus had come to prepare dinner for her, despite her insistence that it wasn't necessary.

The twins weren't even born yet and she was proving to be an incompetent parent.

"I'm starving, Marcellus. Can't you smuggle something in here?"

Sloane had discovered, in the weeks since he'd worked for them, that the mostly quiet man was a culinary genius and a gentle giant. He was built like a linebacker but wore his weight well.

"Benji would kill me." His kind smile always warmed her, mostly because of its rarity. Marcellus's expression seldom revealed emotion. "You'll be asleep in a few hours. Then tomorrow you can eat whatever you'd like."

"You're lucky I'm hooked to this IV. Otherwise, I'd try to turn you upside down until a piece of that beef jerky you've always got stashed on you shakes loose."

Now the man chuckled, a deep rumble that filled the room. She was pretty sure it was the first time she'd ever heard Marcellus laugh.

"Guilty." He patted his breast pocket and smiled. "But the doc says no food for you tonight, so guess what? No food for you tonight. I promise to make up for it once you're cleared to eat again and you and the babies are safe and sound. And you will be, because everything is going to be fine. Okay?"

Sloane nodded, rubbing her belly. She was glad to feel Bailey and Beau moving more than they had been during the preterm contractions.

"Thank you for bringing me here, but I'm sure you have other clients you're supposed to be taking care of today. I don't want to keep you from whatever you had planned. I'm in good hands with Dr. Miller, I promise."

"I'm not leaving here until Benji or your mom arrive." Marcellus's stony expression had returned, though his eyes twinkled.

"I'm here." Benji rushed into the room and went directly to her bedside. He clutched her free hand and clasped it between both of his. "Is everything okay? Are you all right? Are the babies?"

Sloane explained everything as the doctor had explained it to her. They were trying to stop her early labor so she could get as close as possible to bringing the twins to term. But they were preparing the baby's lungs, just in case.

Benji thanked Marcellus profusely. Once the chef was gone, Benji sat beside the bed. He held her hand in one of his, the other gently pressed to her abdomen.

"Are you sure you're okay?"

Something about the sincerity with which he asked the question crumbled the walls of bravado she'd erected.

"No, I'm terrified." She wiped away tears. "If anything happens to them—"

"It won't. I promise." He kissed her hand.

It was a promise he had no power to keep, but

she appreciated his confidence in making it just the same.

Somewhere along the way she'd come to need him. Not because of what he could do for them, but because of quiet moments like this.

Benji was here, and everything was going to be all right. That was enough for now.

Benji checked the calendar. Sloane's preterm scare had been three weeks ago. Since coming home, she'd been on complete bed rest.

He'd convinced her to sleep in his room so he could monitor her at night. Sex wasn't an option while she was on bed rest, so it seemed to relieve her of any anxiety about spending the entire night in his bed.

They'd read, watched TV and chatted every night until she finally drifted off to sleep. He'd held her in his arms and rubbed her belly. He'd felt the twins growing stronger as they moved inside her.

Nothing would've convinced him that he'd be this man, doting over two unborn babies and falling harder and deeper for the woman carrying them.

He cradled Sloane to him. The scare they had a few weeks before had turned him inside out.

What if something had happened to her or to either of the twins?

Neither he nor Sloane had planned this, but she'd been the only woman he'd ever really wanted. He'd known that since he was ten years old. Now that he had her back in his life again and they'd been given this incredible gift, he wouldn't squander the opportunity. He'd do whatever it took to convince her that they should be together, if only for the sake of the twins.

A gush of wetness spread beneath him and Sloane awakened with a gasp.

"Oh, my God. My water just broke. It's happening. We're going to have the babies."

His heart raced and panic gripped his chest, but she needed him to be her strength. She and the twins were counting on him.

Benji kissed her ear and squeezed her tight. "It's okay, baby. Everything is going to be all right. I promise."

It was a promise he kept. Twelve hours later he held Bailey and Beaumont Bennett in his arms.

Six

Sloane was hungry and exhausted. She'd never done anything harder than giving birth to the twins. But as she watched Benji standing by the window, rocking their son in his arms and telling him how glad he was to finally meet him and his sister, it was worth every single moment of pain, exhaustion and terror.

There had been a moment, after she'd delivered Beau, when she'd thought she wouldn't make it. That she couldn't hang on a minute longer. She was in pain and terrified as the doctor reached in and tried to turn Bailey so she'd come out headfirst. Benji had been there, had kissed her and held her hand. He'd whispered in her ear that she was stronger than any woman he'd ever met and assured her she could do this.

"Just hang on a little longer," he'd told her, "and you'll be able to meet our daughter."

He'd breathed with her through the pain. Encouraged her to push once it was time again. Praised her once she'd safely delivered Bailey, too.

She held her daughter, inhaling her sweet scent as she kissed her little forehead. Then she glanced lovingly at the father of the two incredible miniature human beings she'd just given birth to.

Now Benji was rocking Beau, who'd gotten a bit fussy, and singing "Hush Little Baby" in the same deep, throaty, hypnotic drawl that had captivated her the night they'd made the twins.

Her eyes burned with tears, and an involuntary smiled tightened her cheeks. This man was beautiful and sweet. Loving and generous.

Benji still embodied the essential heart-melting qualities she'd loved about him when she'd known him as the sweet kid who was her best friend's little brother. Now, though, there were the new and unfamiliar elements of Benjamin Bennett, the fine, grown-ass man she couldn't seem to get enough of.

As she watched Benji softly singing to their son, her heart felt as if it would burst. There was a part of her that wanted nothing more than to curl up in his arms, holding their beautiful twins. Another part of her feared what would happen once the glow wore off and they were just two people struggling to raise demanding infants.

There was an old, floral photo album in her mother's cabinet with a picture of her father, holding her in his arms and smiling as if he were the proudest father in the history of Magnolia Lake. Yet, her memories of him were of a man who resented her, a man who'd had no interest in being a father and a husband.

She wouldn't put Benji in that position, wouldn't take a chance on waking up one morning and seeing that kind of bitterness in his eyes.

"He's finally gone back to sleep." Benji grinned proudly as he returned Beau to the clear acrylic bassinet marked Bennett, Beaumont. "How's our girl?" He nodded toward Bailey, dozing in Sloane's arms.

"I fed and burped her, and she just fell asleep."

She handed the baby to Benji, and he tenderly kissed the infant's cheek before laying her in her own designated bassinet.

Benji sat in the chair beside Sloane's bed and squeezed her hand. "You were amazing today. What you did... God, I'll never make the mistake of thinking that men are the stronger sex."

"Thank you for being here." She kept her gaze on their joined hands, afraid of getting lost in his deep brown eyes. "I couldn't imagine trying to do this without you." She finally met his gaze. "You were pretty amazing today, too."

Benji cradled her cheek and smiled, pressing a soft kiss to her lips.

"Enough of that, you two. That's how you ended up with these two gorgeous babies in the first place." Abigail Sutton swept into the room, a big grin on her face.

She'd been at the hospital earlier, but she'd had to leave to take Sloane's grandfather to a cardiologist appointment.

"Hey, Mama." Sloane lay back on the pillow, reluctantly pulling away from Benji's touch. "How'd Granddad's appointment go?"

"The cantankerous old thing will probably outlive all of us." She kissed Sloane on the forehead, then crossed the room to give Benji a hug. "He wanted to be here, but after the drive there and back, he was tuckered out."

Her mother was a terrible liar, but Sloane appreciated the effort. Sloane still couldn't shake the look of disappointment on Atticus Ames's face when she'd returned to Magnolia Lake to tell them about her pregnancy. He wasn't happy that she'd unwittingly followed her mother's path. Learning that Benji Bennett was the father had only solidified that stance.

She'd given up trying to please the old man a long time ago. Still, his abject disappointment hurt.

"The twins are sleeping," her mother complained, taking a seat on the sofa near the window. "I was hoping to hold them."

"Go right ahead," Benji said, just as Sloane was going to ask her to let them be. He winked at her. "Your mother came a long way to see the twins. I don't think it will hurt for her to hold them for a bit."

Sloane sighed and gave a reluctant nod.

Her mother moved to the sink and washed her

hands up to her elbows before standing over the sleeping infants in their bassinets, trying to decide which one to pick up first.

"How about if Grandma visits with you first?" She carefully lifted Bailey from her bed and cradled her in her arms.

The girl made only the slightest indication of being perturbed by the move before falling back asleep.

"She's beautiful. The spitting image of you as a newborn." Abigail Sutton beamed as she held little Bailey in her arms.

"Really? I'd love to see Sloane's baby pictures." Benji grinned, obviously amused by the prospect.

"Please don't trot those out." Sloane groaned. "We'll take your word for it."

"Not me." Benji chuckled. "I need to see proof."

Sloane shifted the pillow behind her back as her mother started to coo at her brand-new granddaughter, quickly getting lost in a baby-talk conversation with the sleeping infant.

Sloane lowered her voice and leaned closer to Benji. "That reminds me… I know you said that you trust me, and I appreciate that, but I won't object to a paternity test to prove that the twins are yours."

He shifted his glance to where Abby sat, oblivious to their conversation as she cooed at her granddaughter. His smile hardened into a straight line, but he didn't respond.

"It's okay." She ran her fingers through her hair. "I realize that you need to do this for your own peace of mind and to settle any doubts your mother and Delia have."

The mention of his mother and sister elicited a deep frown that marred his handsome face.

God, Beau looked so much like him. Same mesmerizing brown eyes and strong chin.

"No." His tone conveyed absolute conviction, but something in his tortured expression belied the certainty in his voice. "What my mother and Delia believe or don't is their problem. We don't need to prove anything to them."

"But if it would ease their minds and erase any doubt, why not?"

"Because I don't need it. I know Beau and Bailey are mine. I could feel it the instant I looked into their eyes." He looked back at her. "Data and numbers are essential to my work, but the reason

I've been successful is because I always trust my gut." He patted his stomach. "I know the truth in here. I trust that feeling. And I trust you. I only wish you'd do the same."

"I'm trying." Sloane turned her attention to her hands, perched on her still-swollen belly. "I really am."

"That's all I ask." He squeezed her leg, then stood, turning to her mother. "I'm going to get a real cup of coffee. I don't think I can tolerate another drop of that dreck from the cafeteria. Can I get you anything, Ms. Sutton?"

"We're family now," her mother said, returning Bailey to her bassinet and moving toward Beau's. "Call me Abby. And yes, I'd love a cup of coffee. Nothing fancy. Just black with a couple of packets of sugar."

"Yes, ma'am... I mean...yes, Abby." He leaned over and pressed a chaste kiss to Sloane's forehead, as if he was a nervous teenage boy pinning a corsage on her chest on prom night beneath the watchful eye of her gun-toting grandfather.

He was adorable.

Benji pressed a quick kiss to the forehead of his infant son, lying in Abby's arms, and then left.

"I can't believe that handsome man was once little Benji Bennett." Her mother grinned, sitting beside her and rocking Beau, already sleeping, in her arms. "And I can't believe you're not trying to get him to marry you. He's obviously fond enough of you, he adores these babies and he can give you anything you'd ever want."

Was that what her mother wanted for her? To be with a man who was simply "fond enough" of her? Both she and her mother had married men who were "fond enough" of them, though they'd married for very different reasons.

She'd run off to Nashville with Allen Dickson not long after her eighteenth birthday. He was a session musician who played electric guitar like he'd been born with the thing in his hands. They'd bonded over their common interests—escaping their dysfunctional families, finding careers in the music industry and putting Magnolia Lake firmly in their rearview mirror.

Once those shared grievances were stripped away, there was little substance to their relationship, and they wanted different things from life. Allen had wanted to settle down and start a family. But what he'd really meant was that she'd settle down and raise the kids while he spent the majority of the year on the road, touring the world with one musician or another.

Eventually, her marriage to Allen had ended, like her parents' had. It was a mistake she wouldn't repeat, especially now that she had Beau and Bailey to think about.

"We both know better than most that marrying a man for money isn't the smart move." Guilt tugged at Sloane when her mother's expression deflated. She shook her head. "Sorry, Mama. I shouldn't have said that. I'm just really tired. Maybe now isn't the best time to discuss this."

"Maybe not." Abby Sutton nodded once and turned her attention back to her sleeping grandson. "But there is one thing I want to say... Benji ain't nothin' like your daddy. He's a sweet boy, and he clearly loves Beau and Bailey."

"I know, Mama." Sloane was tired, and she just wanted to sleep. "But it's just not that simple."

We both know better than most that marrying a man for money isn't the smart move.

Benji had gone back to Sloane's room to ask if she'd like him to bring her some real food. Now the words he'd overheard played in his head again and again as he made his way to the parking garage.

After all they'd been through—their history together, the last months of her pregnancy and the birth of their precious twins—was that all she saw in him? That he was a man with money?

Supporting Sloane through the delivery and witnessing the birth of their children was the most amazing experience of his life. He'd been left with a profound connection to her. He thought she'd felt the same. Was he simply seeing what he wanted?

Benji left the hospital, picked up coffee for himself and Abby, then grabbed some food.

He obviously hadn't convinced Sloane that she and the twins were his family as much as his parents and sister were. Not wanting to pressure her, he'd been too subtle, too laid-back.

Time for a bolder approach.

He pressed the voice-command button in his vehicle. "Dial Kamilla Price."

When Benji returned to the room, Abby was holding Bailey again, who'd awakened in his absence. Sloane was breastfeeding Beau. The pained look on her face indicated that the process wasn't going well.

"Everything okay?" he asked her as he set Abby's cup of coffee on the table beside her. She thanked him.

"Other than the fact that I'm questioning whether this one was born with teeth—" she nodded toward Beau in her arms "—everything is good." She sniffed the air and looked at him hopefully. "Please tell me that's a Kick-Back Burger and Rocky Top Potato Skins from Calhoun's."

He lifted the grease-stained bag with a slight grin. "What else?"

"Thank God. It wasn't the epidural that made me queasy, it was that food they were trying to pass off as edible," she grumbled. Then she grimaced in pain. "Ouch, ouch, ouch. Take it easy, Little One. Mama's gonna need those when you're done."

Benji's face flushed with heat. He cleared his throat. "I'll save it for when you're done." He avoided the chair beside the bed and sat next to Abby on the sofa instead. "Got something for you, too, Abby. I guessed, so I hope you like it."

"That's mighty thoughtful of you, Benji. I'm grateful for whatever you brought. I'm not picky, so I'm sure it'll be just fine."

He nodded, glancing at Sloane and Beau, hoping everything would be just fine.

Seven

In the week that Sloane had been in the hospital with the twins, Benji's Range Rover SVAutobiography had arrived from Seattle. As they drove the final stretch of road home from the hospital, she looked over her shoulder in the baby mirrors perched over each twin in the back seat. They were both still asleep. Good.

Maybe she could get in a long nap before they both woke up hungry. Breastfeeding was a struggle, but Benji had been encouraging. He'd even hired a lactation consultant, which she honestly hadn't known was a thing. The nurse and mother of four—including a set of twins—had shown her how to breastfeed the twins simultaneously using a double football hold and a twin nursing pillow. Sloane was still less than confident.

"Everything okay?" Benji tapped her leg, drawing her attention back to him. He'd been wearing the same big grin from the moment the doctor had released them from the hospital. She only wished she felt as ready as he did to begin this thing in earnest. To be the full-time parents of two little people who were dependent upon them for everything.

This was something she couldn't afford to screw up. The stakes were much too high.

It had been easy to judge her own parents. To play Monday-morning quarterback and point out all the ways in which they'd failed. But now that the responsibility was hers, she felt the enormity of the weight upon her, even as her heart expanded with love for the twins and affection for their father.

"Yes." She nodded. "I'm just a little tired. That's all. Hopefully, they'll sleep for a couple of hours so I can get a nap in. Maybe take a hot shower."

Benji frowned, his hands tightening on the wheel. "You said you were tired of lying in bed all day at the hospital. And before that you'd spent so much time isolated at the cabin. I thought maybe you'd want to—"

"You thought maybe I'd want to do what?" She looked up as they approached the cabin. There were five or six cars parked in the long drive.

Sloane recognized several of the vehicles. Delia's car and Rick and Connie Bennett's SUV were notably absent.

"You invited all of these people here as soon as we got home?" Her face flushed with heat and her spine tensed. She raked her fingers through her hair, which was just short of a hot mess after her hospital stay.

"They wanted to welcome you, Beau and Bailey home." He sounded so apologetic that she shifted the focus from her rising anger to how he must be feeling.

Sloane shut her eyes momentarily and took a deep breath. "This was thoughtful of you, Benj. Really."

"Are you sure? Because if you just want to crash, I'm sure they'll understand. I'll explain that I hadn't considered that you'd be wiped out."

"It's okay. I know they're eager to meet the twins. I'll catch up on my sleep later."

He smiled uneasily and nodded. "Okay, great. Because everyone is excited to see you, too."

He pulled in front of the cabin and parked, then came around the car to help her out, refusing to allow her to carry the babies' car seats.

He ushered her inside where her mother, Blake, Savannah and Blake's sister, Zora, warmly greeted her. Her grandfather hung back, seated on the sofa watching television and drinking a beer, wearing his typical frown. Parker greeted her with a curt, but polite nod, then went out to help Blake and Benji bring in the babies in their car seats, her bag and the collection of baby things they'd gathered while in the hospital.

"So how does it feel being a mother now?" Zora asked, guiding her to take a seat on another sofa. "It must seem surreal, right? Especially since you weren't really expecting it."

Sloane had always appreciated that Zora was pretty straightforward. She was similar to her brother Parker in that way. But Parker's directness often made him come off as an arrogant asshole, particularly to those who didn't know him well. Zora's honesty, on the other hand, had the charm and sweetness of the lone girl raised in a house full of boys.

"It was a strange but also kind of wonderful experience." Sloane smiled as her mother and Savannah lifted the babies out of their car seats and fussed over them. "I've been talking to them since the first time I felt them move. But once I saw their little faces…" Tears stung her eyes and her voice broke, but her smile deepened. "Well, it's just really hard to explain."

"Not to me." Savannah sat beside her holding Bailey. "I know exactly what you mean. Davis was completely unexpected and the situation between me and Blake was so dire when I learned I was pregnant. I'm thrilled that everything worked out between me and Blake." She smiled at him adoringly as he helped Benji and Parker carry items to the nursery. "But even if it hadn't, I could never regret having Davis. Blake is the love of my life. My rock. But Davis is my heart. And Blake feels the same."

"You guys seem very happy." Sloane was glad for her friend Blake. He'd had a relationship go terribly wrong a few years earlier, then his relationship with Savannah had nearly blown up when he discovered who she really was—the granddaughter of a man who believed he rightfully deserved half of the Abbott family's distillery.

Despite all of the drama over Savannah having surreptitiously come to town to exact revenge on the Abbotts, they'd managed to reconcile. They'd been mature enough to realize that despite the circumstances, they were meant to be together. And little Davis was a happy surprise.

"Speaking of Davis, where is he?" Sloane looked around the cabin.

"He's with his Grandpa Duke and Grandma Iris. They're spoiling him to death, I'm sure. I guess it pays to be the first grandchild in a family this big."

Sloane watched her mother fussing over Beau. It had been sweet seeing how much she loved and adored the twins. Sloane couldn't ever remember having a relationship like that with her own grandfather. Even in her earliest memories of him, he was wearing the same scowl he wore now as his gaze periodically drifted in her direction.

"My grandfather isn't going to make his way

over here, so I guess I'll go over and say hi to him." Sloane groaned, slowly getting up from the sofa. Her body was still sore.

"While you're gone, maybe Savannah will share the baby since she's already got one of her own." Zora eyed her sister-in-law, who brushed her lips over little Bailey's forehead.

"They're so sweet and they smell so good at this stage," Savannah said dreamily. "Makes me want another one."

"We have a spare, so you can always borrow one." Benji grinned, approaching them. He held a hand out to Sloane. "Hey, come here. Let me show you something."

She slipped her hand in his, conscious of everyone else in the room watching them and of the knowing looks they shared.

"I was just about to say hello to my grandfather. Give me a sec?"

"Sure." Sloane could tell he was trying not to sound disappointed. "Meet me in the nursery when you're done."

She nodded, then made her way across the room to the other sofa and sat beside her grand-

father, who hadn't even looked up to acknowledge her approach.

"Hey, Granddad."

"Sloane." He polished off a little meatball on
a toothpick. Marcellus had outdone himself putting together this little spread for their guests.
"Glad you and the twins made it home and that
you're all okay."

"Thanks, Granddad." She swiped one of the
little meatballs, a fried ravioli and a potato-
cheese-and-onion fritter. They were all foods
that Marcellus knew to be favorites of hers.

Her grandfather gave a disapproving groan but
didn't object. With his dietary restrictions, he
shouldn't be eating half of the food on his plate.

"No more beer," she admonished sternly. "Or
do you want me to text your doctor a picture of
your plate?"

He grunted more loudly this time. "Fine."

It was as close as Atticus Ames was going to
get to saying he loved her, a fact of life she'd accepted and convinced herself she was okay with.
But she was moved by how deeply and immediately her mother had bonded with the twins. And

by hearing Savannah gush about the relationship little Davis had with his grandparents.

Would her life have been different if she'd had that kind of relationship with her grandfather?

"I notice those uppity Bennetts still haven't come around yet." He added an indignant humph. "They always did think that girl of theirs was too good to be friends with you. Connie is probably about to pop an artery because her grandbabies share a bloodline with the likes of us."

"We're surrounded by their relatives and the subject is a sensitive one for Benji, so please refrain from badmouthing them here." Sloane glanced around the room to see if any of the Abbotts had overheard their conversation. "You and Mama can bellyache about my choice of in-laws in the truck on the way home."

"Unless you two stopped at the local magistrate on the way here, them ain't no relatives of mine."

Sloane wondered how long it would take her grandfather to bring up the fact that she and Benji weren't married. She wouldn't take the bait. Not today.

"I have to see what Benji wants." She swayed

a little as she stood. Her grandfather nearly dropped his plate to steady her.

Sloane thanked him and headed down the hall to join Benji in the nursery. If Atticus Ames was willing to sacrifice food that good to keep her from falling, maybe he cared a little more than she thought.

Benji snapped a photo as the nursery door opened and Sloane stepped inside.

Her mouth fell open and she pressed her fingers to her parted lips. A range of emotions played out on her lovely face as she surveyed the room, which had still been undone when she'd been admitted to the hospital to have the twins.

"Oh, my God. It's completely finished." Her voice relayed surprise, but none of the joy he'd expected. "It's beautiful."

Her smile seemed forced as she ran her fingertips along the edge of one of the handcrafted cribs made from locally sourced birch. He'd commissioned them from Zora's best friend, Dallas Hamilton, a local who'd turned his passion for making handcrafted furniture into an international, multimillion dollar business.

Benji had stalled on finishing the twins' nursery because Dallas's commissioned pieces were in high demand, and there was a long waiting list.

The cribs were placed against one wall, separated by a different changing table than the one they'd previously purchased. The shiplap walls had been primed and painted a soft green, and there was a new mural of birch trees, similar to the ones outside of the nursery window. Each of their names was spelled out in handcrafted wooden letters that appeared to hang from the branches of the trees in the mural over their individual cribs. Bailey's letters were painted pink and Beau's were blue. Luxe two-toned silk was suspended over each crib from a rustic cornice, also made from birch. The fabric fanned out to form an elegant little canopy over each crib.

The dressers and changing table were also constructed of matching birch. A luxurious half rocker upholstered in a sage-green fabric completed the furniture in the room. Every piece of furniture in the room was a Dallas Hamilton original.

"I don't know what to say," she said finally, standing in the center of the room and turning slowly as she took it all in. "It's very different from what we'd discussed...but it's beautiful. More so than anything I could've come up with." There was almost a hint of sadness in her voice.

"But you like it, right?"

"It's stunning. How could I not like it?" Her expression was neutral, as if she were stating an indisputable fact. She looked at the cribs again. "What happened to the cribs I bought?"

"They were really nice. But when Zora mentioned that Dallas does custom cribs, I thought it'd be really special to have heirloom pieces made just for them."

"And they're lovely," she agreed, her arms folded. "But you didn't answer my question."

"Since we weren't using them, I thought you'd want them to go to someone who could. I donated them to a women's shelter in Gatlinburg." He took a few steps toward her, trailing his fingers down the outside of her arm. He could feel the tension vibrating off her. "Is something wrong?"

She shook her head, but her eyes looked watery. "They were just wood veneer, purchased at a discount retailer. These are much better."

She stepped beyond his reach and surveyed

the room again with her back to him. As if she needed the space. "How'd you come up with the design?"

"I brought in Kamilla Price, the new interior decorator I told you about. She shot a few ideas past me. I liked them, so I gave her carte blanche to do whatever she liked, as long as she could get it completed before you were released. I'm glad I did. It's better than anything I could've imagined."

Sloane turned to him wearing a polite smile. "Thank you for taking care of everything, but we'd better get back to our company. Beau and Bailey are probably ready for another nap, so we can take their new cribs for a test spin."

She gave him an awkward hug and a kiss on the cheek.

He followed her back to the great room to get Beau and Bailey and they put them down for a nap. Then they returned to the impromptu celebration of the twins' arrival home, both pretending it didn't hurt that Benji's parents and his sister weren't there.

Eight

Sloane lifted her head and checked the clock beside the bed. It was almost noon.

She nearly fell off the bed scrambling to get out of it. The last thing she remembered was feeding the twins in the early morning hours, before the sun rose. But that was several hours ago. Why hadn't she heard their cries?

The proximity of her room to the nursery was the primary reason she'd returned to her own bed rather than sharing Benji's. But since they used state-of-the-art video baby monitors, Benji didn't seem convinced by that argument.

Sloane slid her feet into her slippers and shuffled to the bathroom. Teeth brushed, hair tamed, she made her way to the twins' room next door.

Beau and Bailey weren't in their beds. Her heart raced.

Don't panic. I'm sure Benji has them.

She peeked into his bedroom. He wasn't there. Sloane stepped out into the hall and heard someone singing softly, but it was a female voice. And not one she recognized.

Sloane padded down the hallway quickly but cautiously. She peered into the kitchen. The babies were in their carriers, perched on the kitchen counter. A woman with long, blond hair pulled into a single messy, one-sided braid was singing to them as she stirred something on the stove.

"Who the hell are you, and what are you doing with my kids?" Sloane edged closer, casing the room for something she could use as a weapon in case this chick was some bat-shit crazy stalker who was here to steal her babies.

"Please don't be alarmed, Sloane." The woman held her hands up, her shoulders tensed. "You probably don't remember me, but I'm Olivia Henderson—Mrs. H's niece from Chicago. But please, call me Livvie."

Sloane's hackles went down, but only slightly. She vaguely remembered the girl who'd spent a few weeks visiting her aunt during summers growing up. The woman before her bore no resemblance to the gangly, awkward girl with braces and bad skin who sometimes helped her aunt out at the general store.

"Well, Livvie from Chicago, that doesn't explain what you're doing in my kitchen with my children." Sloane was standing a few feet from the woman. She'd quickly surveyed the twins to make sure they were fine. They both seemed content.

"Maybe it would be better if Benji explained."

"Since he's not here and you are, maybe *you'd* better explain." Sloane didn't like the idea that Benji and this woman shared some conspiratorial secret.

"I had an appointment to meet with both of you this morning, but you were sleeping so soundly that he didn't want to wake you."

"If the appointment was with both of us, why is this the first I'm hearing of it?"

Sloane moved in closer, struck by how beautiful the girl was. She was closer to Benji's age than hers. Her blue eyes were stunning, the color of the Caribbean Sea. And her bronzed skin glowed as if she'd spent more than her share of time on a sandy beach. Her teeth were brilliantly white and perfectly straight.

The braces had obviously paid off.

"Benji wanted to surprise you, I think," the woman explained. "He had to make a quick run into town, but he'll be back shortly."

"What was the appointment about?" Sloane pressed. Her tone made it clear she expected a direct answer.

"Surprise." Livvie shrugged her shoulders, her expression racked with apprehension. "I'm your prospective nanny."

"You're my what?" The blood pumped through her veins more quickly.

"Your prospective nan—"

"I heard what you said, obviously." Sloane clenched her teeth. "But Benji and I talked about this. I was clear that I didn't need a nanny."

Sloane pressed a hand to her forehead and paced. She felt hot and cold at the same time and her hands were shaking.

First there was the housekeeper, then a chef and now a nanny?

Was this what their year together would be like? Benji would call all the shots under the guise of surprising her, while completely ignoring her input?

"I'm sure it would've come off better had he been here to explain himself," the girl said apologetically, returning to the stove. She stirred the pot, inhaling the savory scent.

Beau got fussy and started to cry.

"Hello, handsome." Livvie smiled as she turned off the stove.

She wiped her hands on a rag and reached for the baby, but Sloane stepped in and lifted him from his seat.

"Hey there, Bubba. Did you miss your mama?" She cradled him in her arms. The tension drained from her shoulders when one side of his mouth seemed to pull into a grin. Sloane was fully aware that it was probably just gas. Still, the timing of the pseudo smile made her feel much better.

Sloane kissed Beau's forehead and slipped her finger into his little hand. Despite being barely more than one week old, Beau had quite the grip.

"Since I was sleeping, they must've been given the supplemental formula." Sloane didn't look up at the girl. Instead, she smiled at her son, who studied her face with wide eyes. "When were they last fed?"

"I arrived a little before eight o'clock, and I was here for about two hours before Bailey got fussy. Benji fed her, and I fed Beau. I'd say that was around ten thirtyish." Livvie shrugged.

"Not very precise." Sloane met her gaze momentarily before returning it to Beau's. Maybe she couldn't remember whether she was coming or going, let alone exactly when the babies had eaten last, but this woman was purporting to be a nanny. Shouldn't she have a system for tracking such things?

"Actually, there's an app designed to help multiple caregivers keep track of feedings. I planned to download it to my phone as soon as I got a free moment." Livvie grabbed cheese from the fridge and sprinkled a generous amount into the pot on the stove before returning it.

The woman seemed a little too comfortable in the space. As if she already lived there.

"Are you hungry? Benji said savory cheese

grits are your favorite breakfast." She spooned some in a dish. "So I made plenty."

"I'm not hungry right now, but thanks," Sloane said. Her belly grumbled loudly in protest. She pretended not to notice Livvie's smirk.

"Well, I'm gonna have a bowl. If you need me for anything, I'll be right here." Livvie dropped into a seat at the breakfast bar, took a bite and made an exaggerated "mmm" sound.

Sloane's belly grumbled again, and little Beau gave her another smirk.

Okay, so she was a liar, and both her belly and her baby were calling her out on it.

"Maybe I will have a little before it's time to feed them again," she murmured, strapping Beau back in his chair beside his sister.

"Sit down, I'll fix you a bowl," Livvie said with a broad smile.

When Livvie placed a serving of grits in front of her, she tasted it and nodded. "Not bad for a Chicago girl."

Livvie winked. "My mama's from the South, too, don't forget."

Sloane didn't respond, not wanting to get too

friendly with the girl, whom she planned to send packing as soon as Benji returned.

When she'd finished eating, the twins were fast asleep. She didn't want to rely on an expensive nanny or a private chef or a housekeeper. After all, she wouldn't have any of those luxuries once her year with Benji was up. It was better that she didn't get too dependent. But since Livvie was here, and the babies were asleep...

Sloane rinsed her plate and put it in the dishwasher. "They'll probably sleep for twenty minutes or so. Would you mind watching them while I take a quick shower?"

"Keep an eye on these two little angels?" Livvie smiled as if Sloane had asked her to be her new best friend. "I'd be glad to. You go on and take your shower. I'll clean up in here."

Sloane took a shower and washed her hair. When she emerged from the bathroom, she recognized Benji's distinctive knock on her bedroom door.

She opened the door and glared at him.

"You're upset. Let me explain." Benji frowned.

"I'm listening." She tightened her grip on the towel wrapped around her. "But I can't, for the life of me, understand why you'd leave our new-borns with a complete stranger."

"Liv isn't a stranger. She's Mrs. H's niece. We became good friends when I worked summers at the general store." He placed his hands on her shoulders. "But I'm sorry I wasn't here when you awoke. I hope it wasn't too upsetting."

"I thought she was some crazy stalker who'd killed you and was here to take the babies." Sloane pulled out of his embrace and rifled through the dresser drawers for something to wear. "But, hey, other than that, no big deal."

"That wasn't a good look, and you have reason to be upset. I scheduled time for us to meet with Liv this morning, but you were so exhausted you slept in. Then I had an emergency work call, but I needed a document I'd left at the office. I tried to wake you before I left, but you were dead to the world."

"Why didn't you leave a note?"

He retrieved a piece of paper from beneath the glass of water on her nightstand and waved it before handing it to her.

"Oh." Sloane quickly scanned the note, which explained everything he'd just said. She raised her eyes to his, clutching her clothing in one arm. "Why didn't you tell me about the meeting in advance?"

"Honestly?" Benji sat on the edge of the bed. "Because I knew you'd say no if I asked."

"So you simply chose to ignore my wishes." She crumpled the note and tossed it onto the nightstand.

"You didn't want a housekeeper or a personal chef, but I doubt you'd want to live without either of them now." He sighed when she didn't respond. "Look, it's not as if I've already hired her. I just wanted you to get to know Liv. I figured that would make the prospect of a live-in nanny less intimidating."

"I'm not *intimidated* by your little friend in there. I simply don't need her. There are two of them and there are two of us. I think we can handle a couple of infants on our own." She gathered her clothing and slipped inside the bathroom, shutting the door.

"You were exhausted when we arrived home from the hospital yesterday." The exasperation was evident in his voice, despite the door between them. "And today you were practically in a coma."

"But you clearly didn't just contact what's-her-face this morning." She realized she was being childish and petty by pretending not to know Livvie's name, but she didn't care. This was the second instance in as many days of him making decisions where the twins were concerned without consulting her.

It took him so long to respond Sloane wondered if he'd walked away.

"You're right. Livvie and I keep in touch. She graduated a couple of years ago with a degree in early-childhood education. She'd been working at a premier day care in Chicago, but she wanted a change."

"So you just hired her? How do you know they didn't fire her for losing someone's kid or pushing a toddler down the stairs?"

"Again, I haven't hired her, and I won't if you don't give the okay. And I had her background pulled the moment we discussed the possibility."

"Yet, you still didn't think to tell me you were considering hiring her." Sloane gave up struggling into a pair of pre-pregnancy jeans. She opened the door and strode past Benji. She grabbed a pair of leggings from the dresser drawer and put them on instead.

"It was a surprise," he said, as if that made everything better.

"So are ambushes." She turned around to face him, pulling her top down over her still-rotund belly. She folded her arms. "Don't think just because you're handsome and rich and you smell incredible…" For a moment, the point she was trying to make completely escaped her. "Don't think I won't call you out when you're full of shit. You didn't consult me on this because you knew I'd never agree to it."

"Yes, I was pretty damn sure you wouldn't go for the nanny. But I also knew that we needed the help. Just like we needed Caitlin and Marcellus." He sank onto the edge of the bed. "My job has always been to get results. I identify deficiencies and find solutions."

"I've been a mother for all of a week and already you think I'm deficient?" She planted her hands on her hips, her voice wavering slightly. "Thanks for the vote of confidence."

"I'm not saying you aren't doing a good job,

Sloane. But neither of us has ever done this. We have not one but two infants to care for, and we're learning on the fly here. Is it so bad if we have a little help? It's not as if we can't afford it."

He'd mentioned the money again.

A little of the air deflated from her lungs. She remembered her father screaming at her mother that he made the money so he called the shots.

She clenched her fists at her sides. "I didn't have Beau and Bailey so someone else could raise them."

"And what would you have done if you'd been on your own and had to return to work at the end of maternity leave?" Benji didn't wait for her response. "You would've dropped them off at day care every day or hired a sitter. How is this different?"

She hated him a little for being so goddamned smart.

"I would've been doing it out of necessity." She folded her arms, not looking in his direction. "Not because I preferred to sleep in."

"This isn't a judgment of your ability as a mother." He lifted her chin and forced her eyes to meet his. "You've been so stressed. I just wanted to take the pressure off so we'll have time to enjoy Beau and Bailey. That's all."

"Then why do I feel like you've just subcontracted my duties as a mother to someone else?"

He sucked in an audible breath and released it.

"You know that isn't true. You're a great mother."

"Then have a little faith in me. I'll learn to manage on my own. Millions of women do it every day. Our parents didn't have a chef, a housekeeper and a nanny, and we both turned out fine."

Okay, maybe she was only *relatively* fine, but now wasn't the time to split hairs. Especially when she was finally making a few valid points of her own.

"I know this isn't the way you or I grew up, sweetheart. But I won't apologize for having the means to give our kids a better life than we had."

That she understood.

Sloane hated that Benji's money had become a factor in the conversation again, but the truth was, she wanted a better life for Beau and Bailey, too.

"It would've been nice if you'd consulted with

me rather than ambushing me with Goldilocks out there."

"It's easier to ask for forgiveness than it is to get permission." He shoved his hands in his pockets. "Something else I've learned in business. I anticipate the needs of my clients and employees. When I see a need, I fill it. Even though my team might not be on board yet."

"I'm not your client or your employee."

He furrowed his brows. "It was just a comparison."

"I've barely gotten used to living with you and having Marcellus and Caitlin here part-time. Livvie being here takes things to a whole nother level." Sloane felt claustrophobic just thinking about it. "What if I don't like her? What if Beau and Bailey don't like her?"

"Livvie's sweet, and she was great with Beau and Bailey this morning. Give her a chance, like you did with Marcellus. If you don't like her, she goes. No questions asked." When she reluctantly agreed, he kissed her forehead and turned to leave.

"Benji…" She grabbed his arm and sighed. "I don't mean to seem ungrateful, and I appreciate everything you've done. But I'm not used to this…being so dependent on someone else. It feels like I'm constantly adding to my tab."

She hated saying those words. Hated admitting that she'd become like an extra appendage. He wanted the twins in his life and she got thrown into the bargain.

"I'm not keeping a tab, Sloane." He frowned, seemingly perturbed by the implication that he was. "I don't care about the money, and I don't want you to think about it, either. You, Beau and Bailey are all that matter. Got it?"

She genuinely believed that he meant it in the here and now. But would he eventually come to resent her for all the ways she was indebted to him?

"Got it."

Sloane pushed the unnerving thought from her head and followed Benji out to interview Livvie Henderson about becoming their nanny.

Nine

Benji pulled his Range Rover into the driveway of the cabin and parked. His five-day business trip to Japan had been far more successful than he'd hoped and had resulted in an incredible offer, one he'd be crazy to pass up. It was also the longest period he'd been away from Beau and Bailey. Though they'd video chatted nearly every day of his trip, he'd missed Sloane and the twins like crazy.

He hauled his luggage and laptop inside and inhaled the savory scent of a delicious home-cooked meal. If the heavenly aroma was any indication of how the meal would taste, Marcellus had outdone himself.

"I thought I heard you come in." A broad smile spread across Sloane's face when her eyes met his. "I just put the twins down after feeding them, but they're awake, and I know they'll be glad to see you."

He met her in the middle of the room and kissed her softly on the lips, something he hadn't done in a long time.

The twins had turned three months old the day before he'd left for Japan. Those months had been a blur of feedings, diaper changes, doctor's appointments and incredible firsts. And despite that first rough week after the birth of the twins, he and Sloane had grown closer through it all.

"God, you're a sight for sore eyes." He grazed her cheek with the back of his fingers and inhaled her scent, as fresh as sunshine and summer flowers. Her mop of dark curls was still damp from the shower. She wore a short, belted, button-down dress. It was casual. Nothing fancy, but it hugged her ample curves in all the right places.

"I'll bet you say that to all the mothers of your children." She grinned, adding, "Just kidding," before he could object. Sloane took his hand and led him toward the bedrooms. "Come on. I've got a surprise for you."

His heart thumped a little faster in anticipation. She'd welcomed his kiss and embrace for the first time in months, so clearly she'd missed him. Did that mean she was ready to resume their physical relationship?

Sloane stopped at the twins' room instead, easing inside quietly in case they were asleep.

They weren't. Beau saw him first. He smiled and made a little gurgling noise, slobber rolling down his chin and cheek.

"There's my boy." Benji picked him up, remembering when he'd thought any slobbering child was too gross to touch. Now he leaned in and kissed his son's sloppy cheek without reservation. He gave the boy his finger and let him squeeze it.

"He's gotten stronger." Benji was endlessly amazed by the twins' rapid advancement. It seemed as though they hit some new milestone every day, which was why he'd hated to miss an entire week with them.

"I discovered that when he caught a strand of my hair a couple of days ago." She picked Bailey up, kissed her forehead and handed her to Benji, too.

He sat down in the wide half rocker with both the babies in his arms, talking to them in soft, cooing tones. Though, at Sloane's insistence, he avoided gibberish baby talk.

"What is it?" He couldn't help smiling when he caught a glimpse of Sloane standing in the corner staring at them.

Her eyes shone. She swiped a finger beneath the corners of her damp eyes. "Nothing's wrong. They missed you. I could tell. And they seem so happy to see you. Even at this age, it's obvious how much they love you. I can't believe I ever considered not telling you about them." She shook her head, suddenly choked up with emotion. Her cheeks were wet with tears.

"Don't beat yourself up over something neither of us can change." It was a thought that often plagued him. One he'd rather not explore.

She wiped at her face angrily. "I need to get started on the fried pork chops and check on my macaroni and cheese."

"Wait, you cooked?"

He didn't mean to sound so shocked. But the

truth was, despite her early objections, she'd become quite fond of Marcellus and had fallen in love with his cooking. Even on the weekends when Marcellus wasn't there, they barely ever cooked. He usually ordered something.

"Still don't trust my cooking?" she teased, one hand on her hip.

"No, it's not that. It's just that I know how much you love Marcellus's cooking. He usually makes us something for Friday night."

"I know, but today I didn't want him to cook. I asked him to walk me through cooking dinner. We've been doing that a lot lately, since I have more time on my hands with Livvie being here and everything."

A smile curled the edge of his mouth and she wagged a finger at him. "Don't you dare gloat. It's still way too soon for that."

"I don't know. I'm starting to get a little jealous of Marcellus. I'm beginning to think that aside from Beau here, he's your favorite man in this house."

Her eyes twinkled, and she tugged her lower lip between her teeth as the edge of her mouth turned up in a sensual smile. "We'll see how things go tonight."

She winked at him and laughed as she sashayed from the room.

Benji finally forced himself to push back from the table once his stomach was so full the top button of his khakis was in danger of shooting across the room. Sloane had made juicy, tender fried pork chops, mouthwatering macaroni and cheese, moist, delicious corn bread and spicy collard greens. She served it with chilled sweet tea spiked with King's Finest Bourbon and served Tennessee Jam Cake.

"You put your foot in that meal, girl." He patted his gut, barely able to move. All he wanted to do now was sit on the sofa and catch up on his favorite TV show until he faded into a food coma.

"Thank you?" She laughed, injecting a singsong inflection at the end of the phrase. "That's one of those uniquely Southern phrases I completely understand, but I always think to myself... God, that sounds incredibly gross."

Benji chuckled, pulling her onto his lap and wrapping his arms around her. "Well, it was a damn fine meal, babe. And I'll say it any way you'd like."

"How about like this?" She leaned in, a mischievous smile on her face, and pressed her lips softly to his.

He splayed one hand against her back, desperate to erase the space between him and those lush curves.

She parted her lips to him and he licked the inside of her mouth, savored the taste of Tennessee Jam Cake and sweet tea—hers without bourbon.

Her soft moan made him as hard as steel. His body ached with the desire for her that had been coursing through his veins these past months without release.

His hands moved to the front of her dress as he fumbled to undo the buttons, which were far too large for the buttonholes for his liking.

He could have hiked up her dress and reached underneath it, but he wanted to see every inch of the body he'd grown to love so. To feel the weight of her firm breasts in his palms and soothe the nipples that had suffered such abuse in the weeks after the twins were born and just learning how to latch onto their mother. He wanted to worship her gorgeous body from head to toe with his tongue and then start all over again.

He'd unbuttoned the uncooperative garment down to her navel when the unmistakable cry of their son blared from the baby monitor sitting on the table behind her. The sound was soon followed by the quieter, more delicate cry of his little princess.

Sloane broke their kiss and sighed, pressing her forehead to his. "So much for the after-dinner cordial I had in mind."

He laughed hard, a belly laugh that reminded him that he'd stuffed himself like a Christmas hog. "Adorable little party poopers."

"Those are your children." She pointed a finger at him. "It's time for their next feeding, so I'll go and get them. Just leave the dishes, I'll take care of them when I'm done."

"You cooked. It's the least I can do. Now go ahead before my poor babies get laryngitis."

She stomped her foot, stood ramrod straight and saluted him before saying in the sexiest voice he'd heard her use to date, "Anything for you, Captain."

He laughed heartily and slapped at her bottom

while she skittered away. Then he collected the dishes and carried them to the kitchen.

Damn. He'd been bamboozled. The food had been delicious, but Benji was pretty sure every dish they owned was in that sink, many of which required hand washing.

He turned on the water, rolled up his sleeves and got to scrubbing. At least he'd burn some of the calories he'd just consumed.

Sloane sat in the chair in the nursery and breast-fed both the twins. She hated to admit it, but she didn't know what she'd have done without the lactation consultant Benji had hired. In fact, she couldn't imagine having done any of this without his support.

The financial support was appreciated, of course. After all, it cost a small mint to clothe, feed and diaper one baby, let alone two. But the money came a distant second or third to the emotional and physical support Benji so willingly gave.

They were a team.

It wasn't a platitude, it was a fact. Benjamin Bennett wasn't just a good man, he was an amazing father and an incredible partner. Perhaps the circumstances weren't ideal, but she couldn't imagine herself going through this experience with anyone else.

She loved being a mother to the twins. Loved growing into this crazy life with Benji by her side. Sloane honestly didn't think she could blame it on the hormones anymore, but nothing brought her to tears like seeing Benji interact with their son and daughter or watching how they reacted to him.

It was love, in its purest, rawest form.

But nearly as quickly as she was overcome with joy over her life with Benji and the babies, she was gripped by the throat with fear.

What would happen when the novelty of being a father wore off? Would he resent her? Would he resent the twins?

Part of her realized it was an irrational fear. Benji wasn't her father and shouldn't be judged by his standard of failure. Still, that fear had appointed itself as guardian of her heart. And it seemed safer to let it do just that.

Ten

Benji's eyes fluttered open. His neck was stiff and his body unusually warm. The light from the television flickered over the otherwise dark great room of the cabin. His left arm, partially numb, was pinned between the back of the sofa and Sloane's sleeping form nuzzled against his chest.

He glanced around the room. The twins were sleeping in the double bassinet against the wall. His gaze swept the rest of the room and a soft smile curled the edges of his mouth. When they'd first moved in, the cabin had been a high-end bachelor's getaway. Now it looked like a baby-goods store had exploded and the random pieces had landed around the space.

Yet he was completely content with how the place had changed. It was warmer, more lived in. Now, it wasn't just a cabin. It was a home. Their home.

He gently rubbed Sloane's back. She stopped snoring softly and repositioned herself, but didn't wake up.

Benji slipped from beneath her. He took Beau, then Bailey to their cribs, and turned off the television.

He stood over Sloane. She looked so comfortable, he considered tossing a throw over her and letting her sleep. But as comfortable as the couch was to sit on, she'd be far more comfortable sleeping in her own bed.

He squatted slightly, sliding his hands beneath her and lifting her into his arms, cradling her against his chest. As he carried her down the hall, she lifted her head, her eyes fluttering as she came back to awareness.

"No," she said, halting him in his steps.

"Hey, it's okay," he said gently. "You fell asleep

on the sofa. I'm taking you to your room so you can go back to sleep."

She wiped the sleep from her eyes, her gaze meeting his. "I don't want to go back to my room. I want to go to yours." A sensual smile slowly curved her lips. "And the last thing I want to do is sleep."

Benji stood still, stunned. A part of him wondered if he'd heard her correctly. If maybe she was dreaming, or maybe it was him who was caught inside a dream.

"Make love to me," she whispered in his ear as she cradled his beard-roughened jaw. Sloane pressed her open mouth to his, slipping her tongue inside.

He considered asking her if she was sure, but the insistence of her kiss made it clear that she was fully aware and quite determined.

Benji carried her to his bedroom, stripped off the pesky button-down dress and helped her slip from the pretty but simple nursing bra and panties. Then she helped him out of his clothing until they'd dispatched every barrier between them.

He lay her down, kissed her shoulder, nibbled on her neck and blew a stream of warm air across her skin. "God, you're beautiful. I can't believe how lucky I am."

"I'm glad you're home. We missed you."

"I'm glad Beau and Bailey missed me." He kissed her again and again, his fingertips tracing the stars tatted along her spine. "But I'm especially glad Beau and Bailey's mama missed me. Because I missed her, too."

"Really?" Her lips curved in a mischievous smile, then she sank her teeth into her lower lip. The erotic motion caused his shaft to tighten. "How much did you miss me?"

He reached beyond her, into the nightstand and retrieved a black velvet box, hoping she'd be receptive to the gift he'd deliberated over so intensely.

Benji pulled out the necklace he'd purchased in Tokyo and opened the clasp. He slipped the chain around her neck and let the charm fall between her breasts as he pressed a kiss to her ear. "This much."

He turned on the light so she could see. It was a family necklace with entwined white-gold hearts, each with an emerald suspended near the top of the heart. One heart was engraved with Beau's name and the other with Bailey's. Diamonds were embedded in the remaining surface of the hearts.

She fingered the necklace and turned it so it faced her. Her eyes went wide, and tears spilled down her cheeks. "It's beautiful, Benji. Thank you. I don't know what else to say."

Say you'll marry me were the words that sounded in his head.

"Don't say anything," he whispered. He kissed her, gliding his tongue between her lips as his body moved against hers.

She pressed a hand to his chest. "Benj, don't forget…" She nodded toward the nightstand.

The last time they'd made love she'd been eight months pregnant, so pregnancy wasn't an issue. Now they had to go back to the dreaded barrier between them.

He nodded, reached into the nightstand, sheathed himself and turned the light out again. He kissed her mouth and neck. Trailed kisses down her chest. Ran his tongue over her beaded tips as he reverently held the heavy globes in the palms of his hand. He was gentler with her hardened nipples than he'd been the first time they'd made love. Now he lavished them with delicate kisses and the swirling of his tongue as she squirmed beneath him.

He rained kisses down the valley between her breasts and across her soft belly.

She tensed beneath him, her squirm no longer signaling desire and anticipation, but rather apprehension. As if she were self-conscious about the stretch marks and fullness that the twins had left behind.

"This..." He placed her hand on her belly beneath his as he pressed kisses to the narrow stripes on her skin that were badges of honor. They represented the sacrifice she'd made to have their babies. "This is now my very favorite part of your body. I'll never forget the first time you placed my hand here so I could feel Beau move." He eased their joined hands higher on her stomach. "Or when I first saw Bailey's little shoulder right about there."

He released her hand and kissed lower, to the edge of the small patch of curls over her mound before gliding his tongue along the slick, swollen flesh.

"Or watching you give birth to our children from here." He licked her again. She shivered beneath him and made a little humming sound that made him so hard it hurt. "Then again, maybe this is still my very favorite part."

Wrapping his arms around her thighs, he spread her open with his fingers and delved inside her, licking, sucking and teasing her until she shattered on his tongue. She tensed, her body convulsing as she slowly came down.

Benji kissed his way back up her body, enjoying the way she tensed and relaxed in response to each kiss as she shivered beneath him.

Gripping the base of his shaft, he glided the tip between her slick folds. Something in his chest roared at the delicious feeling of being inside her again. At the way he felt, when she called his name.

Be gentle. Take it easy.

It was their first time together since the birth of the twins, and he didn't want to hurt her. He desperately fought the urge to go hard and fast. Battled the driving need for release after months of not having her.

He strained to move his hips slowly. Deliberately. Despite the fire that burned inside him, screaming for release.

Her body softened beneath him as she moved with him, her fingers digging into his hips. Her breath quickened, coming in hot little pants that made him think about all of the naughty things she could do with that mouth. And how much he'd enjoy them.

He tensed his muscles, trembling as he squeezed his eyes shut and tried to slow his ascent toward climax. He was determined to bring her over the edge one more time. To give her body the intense pleasure it deserved.

Benji lifted her legs higher, changing the angle of entry, grinding his hips slowly and intensifying the friction against her swollen clit.

She cried out his name as she stiffened and her inner walls clenched and unclenched around his heated flesh. He released a primal groan of his own, his back arching as he plunged deeper inside of her.

He hovered above her for a moment, both of them panting as they caught their breath and came down from the peak they'd just been driven to.

He would happily spend the rest of his life making love to this woman. Showering her with gifts.

Raising their family together. And he'd never been prouder in his life than he'd been the day their twins were born. Or more content than he'd been falling asleep on the couch with Sloane and their babies surrounding them.

All of those words came to him as he stared into her eyes. But they lodged at the back of his throat.

The feelings this woman engendered in him raged in his chest. Made him crazy with want and need and the closest thing he'd ever felt to love.

But he'd asked her to marry him and she'd flatly turned him down. Had the months since that rejection changed things for her? Or deepened her feelings for him, the way his feelings had deepened for her?

One night in his bed didn't mean Sloane was suddenly ready to commit to a life with him. Nor did it wipe out the lingering pain and the hint of resentment he worked so hard to hide. But it was a start.

He tumbled onto the mattress beside her and gathered her into his arms. Kissing the side of her face, damp with sweat, he cradled her against his chest, one arm behind his head.

They lay in silence for several minutes before he finally spoke.

"Sloane?"

"Hmm." She sounded like she was in that hazy glow just before sleep.

"Promise me something."

She was silent for a moment as she ran her fingers through the hair on his chest. "If I can."

"Tonight…don't go back to your room. Stay with me. I want to wake up to this beautiful face." He kissed her again.

"I promise," she said without hesitation. He could hear the smile in her voice. "In fact, I was wondering if maybe…" She seemed to lose her nerve momentarily, before she cleared her throat and finally forced the words from her lips. "Would it be okay if I moved in here with you?"

His heart thumped against his breastbone as the weight of her request registered.

Not wanting to sound too eager, he waited a beat before responding. "Yes, I'd like that very much."

Sloane awakened, sprawled across the king-size bed she'd shared with Benji the night before. He was gone. Now she understood the disappointment of awaking to a cold, empty bed when expecting to still be wrapped in the warmth of a lover's embrace.

She dragged a hand through her hair, wondering just how crazy she'd looked when he got up. Or perhaps her tendency to be a wild sleeper had driven him from the bed.

Sloane sighed, staring at the ceiling, one arm thrown over her forehead. She'd spent the night in his bed. Asked to move into his room. A terrifying move she'd been considering during the final days of his trip.

In the scheme of things, five days didn't amount to much at all. But, during those five days, Sloane had discovered something unequivocally.

She'd missed everything about Benjamin Darnell Bennett.

His smart-ass mouth and nerd-boy humor. His innate sense of when she needed him to take control. The heart-melting love and adoration he had for their babies. His incredible body. His friendship and the unique partnership they shared.

Sloane had tried breaking herself of her growing need for Benji. Tried to convince herself that they were co-parents and they needn't be any-thing more.

But during his first long business trip since the birth of the twins, she'd realized the truth. She wanted to be with Benji, but only if he truly loved her, not because he felt some noble sense of obligation.

Sloane fingered the lovely necklace Benji had gifted her the night before. It was the only item she was wearing besides the sheet she'd pulled up to her chest. Sloane appreciated the necklace, but she appreciated the thoughtfulness of the gift even more.

She'd taken a chance by asking him to make love to her. It had been her way of letting him know she wanted more with him. She wasn't sure how things would end between them, but she was ready to consider taking another step forward in their unconventional relationship.

He'd asked her to stay the night with him, rather than slinking off to her room in the wee hours of the morning. But she'd hoped for something more. That perhaps he'd tell her he had *real* feel-ings for her. Not lust or a boyhood crush, but the kind of true, deep feelings she was slowly realizing she had for him.

But she'd seen the devastating shift that happened in a relationship where one person loved unequivocally, and the other wielded all the money and power. She'd seen how that kind of dynamic eroded not only the relationship but damaged everyone in it. Sloane didn't want that for herself or the twins. Nor could she bear to watch the man she was growing to love turn into a bitter, resentful monster.

Sloane got up, showered and dressed. She was greeted by smiles from the twins as she leaned over their cribs. Beau and Bailey were her main priorities, and she needed to focus on them.

She'd keep her feelings for Benji to herself for now.

Eleven

Sloane inhaled deeply, her stomach in knots, as Benji pulled into the driveway of Blake and Savannah's home. Benji seemed to instinctively realize how stressed she was. He threaded their fingers together.

"Relax. It's only Blake and Savannah. We're going to have a great time."

"Of course." She shrugged, as if she didn't have a concern in the world about their lunch date slash playdate.

Sloane glanced over her shoulder where Beau and Bailey lay asleep in their car carriers. The motion of the SUV seemed to put them both to sleep instantly.

At five months now, the twins were already starting to get so big, and they each had their own distinct personalities.

They parked and got the twins out of the car, then Benji went back to get their portable play-pen. Blake and Savannah's little boy, Davis, was now nearly eighteen months old and fascinated by the "babies," which he said often and glee-fully. He was clearly glad not to be the baby of the family anymore.

They fed the children and shared a delicious meal prepared by Blake—who, Sloane was learn-ing, was quite the cookbook aficionado. He'd prepared a roasted vegetable antipasto plate, a delicious salad and the best eggplant parmesan she'd ever eaten, all served with a lovely Chianti she couldn't have because she was still breast-feeding. For her, there was a yummy hibiscus ginger punch instead.

Once the kids were down for a nap, the adults were able to move to the beautiful den with two walls of windows—one overlooking the lake and the other the mountains.

She'd agreed to drive home later so that Benji could enjoy Blake's stash of King's Finest Premium Bourbon while they watched a movie. She and Savannah sat on the other side of the room, taking in the pretty views.

"So, how is not-quite-married life?" Savannah's smile was warm and teasing.

Sloane smiled and sneaked an involuntary glance at Benji, who was laughing with his cousin. Her smile deepened. "Things are good. Really good."

"Wedding bells good?" Savannah prodded as she folded one leg over the other and leaned forward in her chair.

Sloane nearly choked on her punch. She covered her mouth and coughed, using the time to formulate her response.

"I don't think either of us has even considered that yet. Not seriously," she added, thinking of Benji's perfunctory proposal when he'd first learned of her pregnancy. "I know that how we're doing things isn't the traditional Magnolia Lake way. But right now, it's working for us."

"Humph." Savannah looked thoughtful as she leaned back in her chair.

Sloane clearly saw the trap Savannah had laid

out, but like a cartoon mouse, she couldn't resist taking the bait.

"All right, I'll bite. What's the humph for?"

Savannah shrugged and sipped her Chianti. "Maybe I'm allowing my own experience to color the situation," she acknowledged, "but what I hear is fear. I couldn't help noticing the deep connection between you two that day we were all at the cabin. Even though you were obviously a little miffed that you'd been ambushed with a party after your release from the hospital."

Sloane frowned. "Was it that obvious?"

"Maybe not to everyone." Savannah laughed. "But it wasn't that long ago that I had a baby myself. I remember feeling gritty and exhausted. I just wanted to take a hot shower, relax in my own bed and enjoy my time with Blake and our baby. I'd probably have had a meltdown if I'd been presented with a party. Believe me, you handled it well."

Sloane breathed a sigh of relief. It was bad enough that Benji's immediate family wasn't part of his and the twins' lives. The last thing she wanted to do was alienate his extended family. The Abbotts had been warm and welcoming to her. The only person who seemed to regard her suspiciously was Parker.

Then again, no one in Magnolia Lake would use the terms *Parker Abbott* and *friendly* in the same sentence.

"The bond between you two seems even stronger now." Savannah nodded toward Benji. "It's obvious how much he adores you and the twins."

Sloane sighed, feeling a little more at ease with Savannah. "I care for him. Very much. Still, there are a lot of issues we both need to work out. One of which is, despite what he says, I often wonder if he'll ever fully trust me since he had to find out about the twins on his own. Sometimes, when he looks at me, I see it, that pain and resentment. Him imagining what would've happened had he not shown up at my place in Nashville that day." Sloane swallowed hard. "It made so much sense in my head when I made the decision. Now it just seems cowardly and selfish. I don't blame him for being angry."

Savannah nodded sagely. "You know the story of what happened between me and Blake and why I really came to Magnolia Lake?"

Sloane nodded apologetically. She hated to

admit that she—and everyone in the town or who had relatives here—had heard the story.

"And yet here we are. Together. Happy. And truly in love." An absent smile lit her eyes as she talked about Blake. Then her gaze met Sloane's again. "I hate to sound like one of those annoying newlywed couples, but I honestly feel… No—" she shook her head "—I know that Blake is the man I was meant to spend my life with. The way we came to be… I'll always bear some pain for my role in deceiving him in the beginning. But if I hadn't come here, hadn't done what I did, there would be no us. And we wouldn't have learned the truth about the role my grandfather played in King's Finest."

Sloane glanced over at Benji. Could they, too, have a happy ending despite their inauspicious start?

"I honestly want to believe that Benji and I could have the kind of relationship that you and Blake have, but…" Sloane looked over at Benji, who seemed to be having a more serious discussion with Blake now. "I don't know. Especially with him being estranged from his family. They didn't even come back to Magnolia Lake this summer the way they typically do. I'm hurt and angry about their reaction to me and Benji. Delia, especially. We've been best friends since we were ten years old. I can't believe she'd think, even for a minute, that I'd ever do anything to harm or take advantage of her brother."

Savannah's hazel eyes were filled with sympathy. She placed a hand on Sloane's arm. "I'm sorry that the Bennetts are being so unfair to you. Iris feels horrible about it," she said, referring to her mother-in-law, who was Benji's aunt. "She's tried talking to her sister, but Benji's mother won't budge."

"I appreciate it. And as furious as I am with Delia and Connie, it's mostly because of what it's doing to Benji. He doesn't like to talk about it, but I can see how much it hurts him." Sloane took another sip of her punch and shook her head. "I hate being the wedge that drove Benji and his family apart. They've always been so close."

"He sided with you over his own family." Savannah looked at her pointedly. "And you think that man isn't serious about you?" The question didn't require a response. "Take things as slowly as you need to. Don't mind busybodies like me trying to rush you to the altar." Her smile widened and they both laughed. "I know Benji has reasons to be hurt, just as Blake did. But if he's trying this hard to get over it, he obviously wants this. Don't give up on him. Give him time. He'll get there."

Sloane hugged Savannah and thanked her.

She didn't know where things would go between her and Benji, but she felt more hopeful about it than she ever had before.

Benji and Blake had volunteered to bundle up the kids, put them in strollers and take Blake's two dogs—Benny the Labradoodle and Sam the greyhound—for a walk around the lake. But the real reason for the walk was that Blake wanted to talk to Benji. It was a conversation Benji wasn't sure he wanted to have, mostly because he already knew he wouldn't have answers to many of the questions his cousin would ask.

Where did things stand with him and Sloane? Were they a bona fide couple now?

The answers were that he didn't know and he didn't think so, though he felt more hopeful that it was possible. As far as he was concerned, it wasn't a conversation worth packing up three children and two dogs.

After they covered the basics, Blake asked him a pointed question. "Do you love her?"

Benji frowned at his cousin.

"Does that mean no, or is it that you think I've broken some unofficial bro code by asking you about your 'feelings'?" Blake made a flourish with his hands when he said the word.

"The latter." Benji stared out onto the lake instead of looking at his cousin.

Blake chuckled. "Well, put your big-boy pants on and try to make an exception just this once." Blake elbowed Benji in his side, then indicated the spit-up dribbling down Beau's chin.

Benji wiped his mouth and secured the blankets around the twins, who both seemed to enjoy the venture into nature. Likely because Livvie often took them for walks around the lake by their cabin.

"Yes," Benji said finally.

"Yes, what?" Blake wasn't going to let him get off with the bare minimum. He was determined to throw a little torture in with his cousinly advice.

"Yes," Benji said, pausing. "I think I love her."

"You *think* you love her?" Blake was like Benny with a bone. For a fleeting moment Benji wanted to knock that self-satisfied smirk off his older cousin's face.

"Anyone ever tell you that you can be kind of an asshole?" Benji gritted the words through clenched teeth, his voice low enough that none of the children could hear him.

Blake laughed harder than Benji thought the situation required.

"Yes," his cousin said. "But usually only people I'm related to by blood."

Now Benji chuckled, too.

"Okay, fine," he said finally. "I do. I love her. I've never felt this way about anyone before. I honestly think I've been in love with her since I was ten years old. When I saw her again at your wedding—God, I thought I'd gotten over that puppy-love crush. But the second I saw her…it was like I'd been hit by a ton of bricks."

"Well, you certainly know the mother of your children better than I do," Blake said, carefully prefacing his next statement. "But the Sloane I've always known is a tough nut to crack. She's got issues with her mom and her dad. She doesn't like to need anyone or anything, and she's slow to let people inside. But if you can ride out the storm and prove that you're worthy, that you won't let her down like so many people in her life have… Man, it's worth it. She's a good person. And you two could be really good together, if you're both willing to work for it."

"That's just it." Benji halted on the path as Blake's house came into view. "I've been trying to show her. There's obviously friendship and affection between us. Fire," he added, his cheeks heating slightly. "I just don't know if she's ready to commit to something permanent."

"Have you told her how you feel about her?"

"I asked her to marry me."

"And she turned you down? When was this?" Blake looked stunned, but when Benji gave him the rest of the details, Blake shook his head and whistled. "Man, no wonder she turned you down. That wasn't a marriage proposal, it was a business proposition. Sloane isn't the analytical kind who would make a decision like that based on logic alone." He patted his chest. "The girl's all heart. If you want her to love you, to really be willing to risk her heart for you, you're going to have to strap on a set and lay it all out there, Benj."

Blake started walking toward the house again, but Benji tugged him by the elbow. "What if she doesn't love me the way I love her? What if she never will?"

"Then it's better that you swallow that bitter pill sooner rather than later," Blake said gravely. "But for what it's worth, I don't think that's it at all. If Sloane is the one for you, just keep showing her how you feel until you're ready to tell her."

Benji nodded and they resumed their final journey back to the house.

Sloane was the woman for him. He was as sure of it now as he had been when he was ten. Only now it wasn't based on a childish infatuation. It was based on something real and true.

Still, sometimes it was hard to turn off the nagging little voice in the back of his head. The one that pointed out that if he hadn't gone looking for Sloane, she might never have revealed the truth. The one that reminded him that if he hadn't made a deal to pay off her family's debt, she wouldn't be with him now. And the ticking of the clock reminding him that in seven months she planned to take their twins and walk away.

Twelve

Sloane sat at her mother's farmhouse kitchen table savoring her first cup of coffee in more than a year. The twins had just turned seven months old and were completely weaned. Sloane's grandfather was mesmerized by the twins—both of whom adored him. And Bailey had a special bond with the old man. The first time Atticus Ames held her in his arms and she tugged at his wiry gray beard, she'd had him wrapped around her tiny little digit. And she'd brought her big brother along for the ride.

Now he couldn't get enough of the twins. He visited them often. He even accompanied Livvie when she took the twins for their daily walk around the lake in their double stroller, weather permitting.

Beau was crawling across the floor, playing with one of the countless musical baby toys that drove Sloane crazy and made her consider sabotaging them.

Bailey was in her favorite spot—standing on her great-grandfather's lap and trying to swipe his glasses off his face. She was fast and occasionally she succeeded.

For which the old man never so much as gave her a sideways glance. Instead, his deep chuckle filled the room. "You got 'em again, Bailey. Paw-Paw has got to be quicker."

"He was never that kind and understanding with me," Sloane grumbled, keeping her voice low enough not to travel the short distance to the family room where her grandfather and the kids were. She poured a generous amount of creamer into her second cup of coffee. "If it was me, I'd be on the floor doing baby push-ups or something."

"Honey, you really shouldn't exaggerate about your grandfather that way. He wasn't as bad as you make him out to be. He loves you and you know it."

"He's always had a damn funny way of showing it," she muttered under her breath, and nibbled on another one of her mother's homemade cinnamon rolls. Which didn't help her goal of losing that last fifteen pounds of baby weight.

Okay, maybe it was twenty. But Marcellus was a darn good cook.

"I know he was hard on you, but he regrets that." Her mother sighed heavily, taking another small bite of her cinnamon roll. "I suppose I'm the one to blame for that. He felt he failed with me, so he was determined that you were going to be that perfect little girl that I wasn't." Her mother's voice was small, her eyes sad.

Sloane reached over and squeezed her hand. Being a mother herself had given her new perspective on the enormous duty of raising a child—or in her case, two. Her mother had been little more than a child herself when Sloane was born. She'd done the best she could with the skills and experience she had.

Sloane didn't agree with the choices her mother had made, but she respected the fact that she'd made those choices because it was what she felt she needed to do in order to take care of her.

"Granddad's grand plan for me didn't exactly work out." Sloane forced a bitter laugh. "I guess we're both incorrigible."

"Wouldn't say that exactly." He was standing over them holding Bailey, who chose that moment to say, "Ma, Ma, Ma!"

"Nice, Bailes. You couldn't have given me a heads-up *before* you guys got in here?" Sloane teased her daughter. Bailey laughed, whether she understood what was going on or not.

Sloane's mother got up from the table, a sad smile on her face. "I'd better check on Beau. I'll take Bailey, too." She put Bailey in the playpen and then picked up Beau, who was absolutely a grandmama's boy. His face spread into a gummy smile, showcasing two top teeth and one on the bottom.

Her grandfather sat at the table, both of them quiet until Sloane couldn't take the silence between them anymore.

"Look, about what I said, Granddad. I'm sorry. I shouldn't have said it." There, she'd apologized and hadn't lied by saying that she hadn't meant it.

"That's how you feel, and I can't change that." He tapped the table rhythmically. Then he raised his eyes to meet hers. "But I can apologize and try to explain why I was so tough on you."

Sloane tipped her head, her brows furrowed. Who was this contrite man who was putty in the hands of precocious infants and willingly offered apologies?

"All right," she said simply.

"I never got to be that doting grandparent with you because I was as stupid and wrongheaded as Benji's family. I'd insisted that boy marry your mother, but that didn't make me like or respect him. So I kept my distance. Missed most of the first year or two of your life. Never got to bond with you the way I've been blessed to have bonded with these two." He pointed in the direction of the playpen in the other room. "Then when I did come into your life, I could see how smart and determined you were. How much potential you had. I didn't want you to squander it the way I felt your mother had. So I took the hard line. Tried to make you the person I thought you should be. And it only got worse when your father left, because I was trying to be your father and your grandfather. Prepare you for the world."

"And how'd that work out?" Sloane interjected, needing to add some levity to the tense situation.

He shook his head and chuckled bitterly. "Problem was that you and I are too goddamned much alike. You fought me tooth and nail. You were determined to be whoever the hell you wanted to be, which was deliberately the complete opposite of what I wanted for you."

There may have been some truth to both those statements, but she wasn't inclined to admit to either at the moment. Nor was she inclined to give him a you're-excused-for-sucking-as-a-grandfather pass so he could go back to happily playing peekaboo with the twins, as if the way he'd treated her back then was no big deal or as if it hadn't shaped the choices she and her mother had made.

"Why are you telling me this now?" She held back the anger that trembled just below her carefully controlled surface, like only the tip of an iceberg showing above the cold, icy waters that doomed the *Titanic*.

"I only wanted to prevent you from making the mistakes your parents made. I didn't want you to run away from responsibility and family the way your father did. Or go chasing after the wrong men like your mother. But my hard, cold demeanor pushed you away. Prompted you to do both." His voice broke slightly.

When she met her grandfather's eyes, there were tears in them. The sight shook her, like a two-ton wrecking ball crashing against an old, dilapidated building. Suddenly he didn't look like the old man who'd tried to ruin her fun at every turn. He was sad. Broken. Remorseful. None of those were words she'd ever used to describe him.

He pulled a hanky out of his pocket and quickly dabbed his eyes as he shook his head.

"Maybe there's nothing I can ever do to change how you see me. But I can't let you ruin your life and theirs without at least speaking up about it." He stuffed the hanky back in his pocket.

"What do you mean?"

"If your plan is still to take the twins and walk away after their first birthday, it'd be a huge mistake that none of you will likely ever recover from."

"You're being a little melodramatic, Gramps." Sloane's gaze dropped to the cup of cooled coffee in her hands.

"Benji's a good man, Sloane. And he's one hell of a father. Regardless of what brought you two together, you've been blessed with each other and the twins. Don't take that gift for granted." His voice was tender.

In that moment, the dam she'd spent her entire life building around her heart, brick by brick, cracked.

It was jarring to see Atticus Ames in a new light. Yet, it relieved a little of the constant pressure that she'd felt in her chest for as long as she could remember.

Not trusting herself to speak, Sloane nodded to acknowledge that she'd heard her grandfather's wise words. She stayed silent and pretended she didn't feel the wetness that fell from the edges of her eyelashes and stained her cheeks.

But as for what would happen between her and Benji…that wasn't only up to her.

Thirteen

Benji whistled as he entered the Magnolia Lake Bakery on Main Street in town. The twins were nine months old and had both learned to pull themselves into a standing position on the furniture during their recent two-week visit to his place in Seattle.

He'd run through the house excitedly to tell Sloane, who'd been soaking in the tub, about Bailey's latest feat. By the time Sloane had gotten out of the tub and padded with damp feet into the family room, Beau, who refused to be outshone by his younger twin, had also pulled himself up on the couch.

They'd both been so excited and Sloane, a videographer and editor by profession, had grabbed her ever-present camera to record the twins' latest development.

It was a week later, and while he and the twins were back at the cabin, he'd treated Sloane and her mother to a few days at a luxury spa resort in the mountains, about forty minutes outside of town.

Benji still couldn't stop grinning like a fool. Because all was right in his world. Granted, neither he nor Sloane had said those three little words. Nor had they formalized their relationship. But they were closer to it every day. He could feel it, knew it as certainly as if they'd signed their names to a contract written in blood.

They were a family. He and Sloane recognized that the twins needed them both. And that they needed and wanted each other.

He was ready to take the plunge, to lay his heart on the line and ask Sloane to marry him again. Only this time he'd do it right. Let her know that the reason he wanted to marry her had everything to do with her being a beautiful, intelligent woman who made him laugh and with whom he enjoyed spending time. She was the person he felt closest to in the world, and he could no longer imagine his life without her.

He'd already purchased the perfect engagement ring. He just hadn't decided when and how he'd ask Sloane to be his wife.

"Hey, Park." Benji slipped into his seat and turned over his coffee cup, indicating to Paige, the waitress, that he'd like a cup of coffee.

"You look happier than a pig in slop," Parker remarked bluntly. "I would've preferred it if you weren't so happy this morning."

Benji frowned. He was used to his cousin's odd comments that sometimes bordered on rude, but it seemed harsh even for Parker to say he wished he wasn't so happy.

Shit. This can't be good.

Benji suddenly wondered if he should ask the waitress to top his coffee off with a little bourbon to make whatever hell Parker was about to rain down on him go down a little smoother.

Taking a sip, Benji waited for the strong, piping-hot coffee to hit his system before he asked the next logical question.

"What the hell are you talking about, Parker?"

"I have two things to tell you, and I don't think

you're going to like either of them," his cousin said matter-of-factly.

Benji's heart crumbled in his chest. Parker wasn't given to histrionics. If he indicated that the news was bad, it was. Unequivocally.

"All right, Park," he said after another hit of coffee. He set his mug on the table and met his cousin's eyes. "What is it?"

"Yesterday I stopped into Kayleigh's shop to look for something for my mother's birthday."

"Why would you go to Kayleigh's shop? You don't even like her, and she's certainly no fan of yours." Benji chuckled. Parker and Kayleigh Jemison's love-hate relationship dated back to when they were all kids. Once close friends, he'd chosen the popular kids over her during a very un-Parker-like time in his young life. Kayleigh had never forgiven him and wasn't very fond of the Abbotts in general.

"My mother and sister like her jewelry pieces. They've been requesting them as gifts for the past couple of years," Parker informed him, clearly agitated by the subject. "But that's not the point. The point is that she does like you. Always has.

So she felt the need to make me aware of a few things."

"Such as?" Benji's gut churned. He was already growing weary of this little song and dance.

"Did you know that Sloane's family's farm was *this close* to being repossessed?" Parker peered through a tiny space between his forefinger and thumb.

"Yes."

"And did you know her condo in Nashville was in jeopardy of being repossessed, as well?"

He nodded once, sipping his coffee. "I did. The question is how does Kayleigh know all this? Sloane and her family's finances are their business. Not fodder for this town's gossip mill."

Suddenly he understood Sloane's reluctance to return to Magnolia Lake. The low crime rate and quiet, relaxing pace of life left folks with an awful lot of free time on their hands. Not all of them used that time well.

"Why does any of this matter?"

"Because Sloane gets pregnant by you—a very wealthy man who she just happens to know has always had a crush on her. She hasn't attended a funeral or wedding in this town for years, but she's there at Blake's wedding, knowing you'll be there, and suddenly you two tumble into bed? Does any of this really seem like a coincidence to you, Benj?"

"Why can't it be?" Benji wanted to believe it with all his heart. He could forgive a lot of things, but he wouldn't be able to countenance having been Sloane's "mark." He shook the thought from his head. Sloane wasn't the type. He knew that as well as he knew himself.

"You know my philosophy on coincidences, Benj." Parker drank some of the espresso that kept his intricate mind fueled all day, since the man subsisted on three or four hours of sleep.

Benji did know Parker's theory on coincidences. He also knew how skeptical Parker was about the fact that he and Sloane had gotten together than night and conceived twins, despite using preventive measures.

But he didn't want to hear any of Parker's theoretical bullshit this morning. Benji was only a few steps up the ladder of maturity from plugging his fingers in his ears and singing "la-la-la-la" until Parker got the hint and shut the fuck up.

"You're a smart, sensible guy, Benj. So I know that at the very least, you took a paternity test."

His nostrils flared, and his pulse quickened, as anger filtered through his bloodstream.

He glared at his cousin. "Beau and Bailey are nine months old. Why are you bringing this up now?"

"It's not like I haven't brought it up before," Parker reminded him. "You just weren't receptive. Probably because it was your mother who insisted on the paternity test. But in light of this new information, the question seems valid. I don't suppose I need to ask if you're the reason Sloane and her family are no longer in debt."

"How I choose to distribute my finances is my own damn business." Benji's muscles tensed as he gripped the mug. "You're the chief financial officer at King's Finest, not mine."

"I can't understand why you'd be willing to lay out that kind of cash without irrefutable proof that…" Parker's eyes widened and he pointed a finger at Benji. "You're afraid they're not yours. That this entire world you've built with Sloane is going to come crashing down at your feet like a house of cards."

"Back off, Parker. This is a road you don't want to go down. Trust me."

Parker, who, for all of his intelligence, wasn't the best at reading people, had chosen today to exhibit insight. If he hadn't been the subject of Parker's scrutiny, Benji might've actually been proud of his cousin.

It wasn't that he had any real doubts about the paternity of the twins. Besides his gut feeling, both Beau and Bailey possessed plenty of his physical features. But perhaps there was a tiny, dark part of his heart that entertained the accusations his mother had made against Sloane.

"And despite her joking with your sister about needing a sugar daddy to dig herself out of her family's financial mess, you choose to believe this was all just a serendipitous coincidence?"

"Yes."

"Even though Sloane told Kayleigh at the reception that she had *a plan* to get out of debt?" Parker stared at him incredulously and pushed his expensive designer glasses up the bridge of his nose. "Seems to me like that plan was you."

"Dammit, Parker." Benji slammed his fist on the table and the dishes and silverware clattered.

"I'm only going to say this once, so listen up. Sloane has already admitted that she *and* Delia joked about the sugar daddy thing, well before I sold my company. She was kidding, Parker. I know that's a concept you aren't very familiar with—" he shouldn't have taken that jab at his cousin, but he was more than a little pissed at Parker's determination to "save" him from himself when it came to Sloane "—but she was no more serious about it than Delia was. It was a joke. Would you want people taking everything you've ever said literally, even things you said in jest?"

"I don't generally have time for jesting, so yes." There was zero humor in Parker's response.

Great. Benji had forgotten for a second exactly who he was dealing with. Parker was literal and stone-cold serious about everything. Not that the guy never laughed, but his cousin wouldn't have to worry about laugh lines anytime soon. Parker had little use for humor or sarcasm, which often went over his head.

"Okay, for once in your life, don't apply that question to yourself. Think in terms of the broader population of…you know, human beings." He was usually Parker's biggest defender, but right now he was furious with his cousin.

"And her grand plan for getting out of debt?"

"I don't know." He shrugged. "I only know it had nothing to do with me."

When Parker didn't respond, Benji asked, "We done here?"

"No. There's one more thing. Aunt Connie asked me to relay a message. She wants you to bring the twins for a visit. Whether they're biologically yours or not, you've chosen to raise them. That makes Beau and Bailey her grandchildren, and she wants to get to know them."

"My number hasn't changed." Benji stared out the front window of the bakery onto Main Street. "If she has something to say to me she could always call. Better yet, she could come here and talk to me face-to-face. Show me the same courtesy I showed them. And I'm not bringing the twins to visit her if their mother's not welcome, too."

"Fair enough." Parker drank more of his espresso. "If your family wanted to talk, maybe even apologize, you'd welcome that conversation, right?"

Hurt and anger roiled in Benji's gut. The same anger and frustration he felt when he recalled his family's reaction to his announcement about Sloane and the twins.

He ordered a King's Finest Coffee—one part bourbon, one part cream liqueur, a splash of hazelnut liquor and a whole lot of strong coffee, dressed up with a flourish of whipped cream.

"Well?" Parker was clearly impatient with Benji's reluctance to give him a yes or no response. "Look, I may not be the most sociable guy in the world, but even I recognize the importance of family. As happy as you've been with Sloane and the twins these past months, you're equally torn by how much you miss your own family."

"That was their choice, not mine."

"I know," Parker said quietly. "But you've been at an impasse for months. If they're humble enough to admit they bear some blame in this, would you be big enough to accept it?"

In the beginning, it was a question he wouldn't have needed to think on. The answer would have been a resounding *yes*. But the longer their stalemate had gone on, the more difficult the question had become to answer.

"The twins will be one in a few months. They've never met their grandparents, their aunt or their first cousin." There was a soft pleading in Parker's voice that Benji had never heard before. "That's not how we were raised, Benj. We're family. Yeah, we do stupid things and sometimes we screw up. But we forgive each other, and we move on."

"I'll think about it." Benji shrugged as Paige set the steaming glass mug of King's Finest Coffee in front of him.

Parker's eyes sparked with recognition before returning his attention to Benji. He nodded to something behind him. "You'd better think quick."

Benji turned and looked up as he took his first sip of the frothy, bourbon-laced coffee.

"Hi, Benji." Delia stood over him, her expression pained. "Do you think we could talk?"

Fourteen

Benji narrowed his eyes at his cousin and released a heavy sigh. He returned his spiked coffee to the table and indicated that Delia should take the seat Parker currently occupied.

"Oh, right." Parker jumped up from his seat and reached into his back pocket for his wallet.

"Forget it, Parker." Delia slid into her cousin's recently vacated seat. "This one's on me."

Parker thanked her and grinned. "Hey, Paige, would you mind adding a couple of sticky buns and another cup of coffee to my tab. Delia's paying."

"Cheapskate."

Benji and Delia uttered the word simultaneously. Neither of them laughed, but their expressions softened and Benji saw a flash of one of his big sister's dimples.

"So, you asked for this meeting," Benji said finally, sipping the hot coffee and enjoying the warmth of the bourbon that slowly spread through his chest.

"I'll have one of those, too, Paige." Delia nodded toward Benji's drink.

"Coming right up." The waitress nodded knowingly.

Delia removed her coat before folding her hands on the table and looking up at him.

"Benji, you're my brother, and I love you. I'm sorry for how I handled things. Sloane is…was my oldest, dearest friend." She unwrapped the napkin from the silverware and dabbed the corner of her eyes. "I was hurt that she'd sleep with my little brother and then not even tell me that you were the father of her twins."

He didn't respond, and he resisted the urge to comfort his sister in any way. Delia had been cruel to Sloane, and she needed to feel the pain. To sit there and wallow in the enormity of her accusation against her friend.

"I can't speak for Mom, but I made this entire thing about my friendship with Sloane. That wasn't fair to you or to my niece and nephew. And it wasn't fair to Sloane. She's always been there for me. I should've been able to get past my hurt feelings and do the same." She dabbed her tears again. "Guess it's obvious which one of us is the better person."

Paige set Delia's coffee on the table and gave them both a worried glance before excusing herself.

"I appreciate your apology, Delia, but I can only accept on my own behalf. You'll need to talk to Sloane yourself. I'm sure she'd be glad to hear from you."

A flash of something crossed his sister's face as she shifted her gaze from his and rubbed her ear. There was something she wasn't telling him.

"I miss you, baby brother." Delia's big brown eyes met his again. "And Evie misses her uncle Benji."

"I miss you guys, too." His estrangement from his family had caused many sleepless nights. "How are Mom and Dad doing?"

"Honestly? Mom's miserable and things haven't

been great between her and Dad. It was Dad who finally insisted that we all come here and talk to you. I think he might actually be growing a spine."

"Better late than never, I guess." Benji shrugged. "So they're in town, too?"

"They will be in about an hour." Delia checked her watch. "I arrived last night."

"Thanks for the heads-up," he said. An awkward silence settled over them for a moment.

"Fatherhood looks good on you, Benj. You were a good uncle, but you're an incredible dad." Delia's voice broke and she dabbed at her eyes again.

"How would you know?"

Delia released a heavy sigh and bit her lip. "First, promise me you won't get angry or go back on your word."

"To whom?" There was a sinking feeling in his gut.

"Sloane." Delia whispered her name.

"You talked to Sloane?"

"Not exactly. But she's been talking to me through this private blog where she keeps kind of a video journal. It's one of those mommy blogs where she shares cute little stories about your life together and posts pictures of you guys and the twins. It isn't public, and she doesn't use your real names. She refers to the twins as Little Dude and Buttercup. Sloane sends me the link whenever a new entry is posted."

"Let me see this blog." He held out his open palm.

Delia retrieved her phone, pulled up a website and handed it to him.

Benji scrolled through the photos of Beau and Bailey. Played a couple of the videos showing various stages of the twins' development or Sloane openly gushing about what a good dad he was.

He was angry she'd kept this from him. Trust was already a sore spot in their relationship, and this was one more secret between them. Yet, he couldn't help being moved by the touching things she'd said about him.

He rubbed his jaw as he watched small clips of one video after another. Benji sent the blog link to his phone via text message, then returned his sister's phone. Suddenly the last part of Delia's request came back to him.

"You said not to go back on anything I'd promised her. Does that mean she told you every-thing?"

His sister nodded. "She told me about the condo and the farm. She felt guilty about keeping it from me, and she was afraid that hiding it only made my accusations seem warranted. So she wanted me to know. Even if it meant you would go back on your arrangement, it was a chance she was willing to take. She couldn't bear being the cause of the rupture in our family. Told me to do whatever I wanted with the information."

"Did you tell Mom and Dad?"

"I haven't told anyone. But you know it won't sit well with Mom. She'll think it only proves what she already believed. That Sloane did this for the money."

Gossip was easy to come by in a small town. If his sister said she hadn't told anyone, he be-lieved her.

"I know Sloane wouldn't have put that on the blog."

"No, she included that in the first email to me. I've never responded to any of her emails or calls."

"If you're telling me all this, why not?"

"I wasn't ready to forgive her, and to be honest, I'm still a little hurt. But I miss my friend, and eventually, I'll be ready. But for right now, I knew I needed to reach out to you and make amends."

Delia reached for his hands across the table. She seemed relieved that he didn't withdraw them.

"I know the world sees you as a powerful, successful businessman, and I couldn't be prouder. But part of me still sees that sweet, naive little brother that I need to protect."

"Noted, but I'm a big boy now. I can take care of myself, and you." He gave his sister a faint smile.

"One more thing." Delia took a sip of her coffee. "I know I was dead set against the relationship, but you two seem really good together. I'm pretty sure she loves you just as madly as you love her."

"She tell you that in the email, too?"

"She didn't need to. Your love for her and the twins is apparent in those videos. And the love she has for you... It's obvious when she gushes about you." Delia drank more of her coffee. "I'd love to believe that the primary reason Sloane reached out to me was to salvage our friendship, but the truth is…she did this because she cares deeply about you. You've been living together for a year. Don't you see it?"

He did see that Sloane cared for him, and he appreciated her heartfelt desire for him to reconcile with his family. But he couldn't help feeling she'd betrayed him again.

He'd sworn her to secrecy about their financial agreement. If Sloane had felt so strongly about telling Delia, she should've discussed it with him, instead of going behind his back and hoping for the best.

Benji cared deeply for Sloane, but if they were going to have any kind of future together, he needed to be able to trust her.

Right now, he wasn't sure if he could.

Fifteen

"I could get accustomed to living like this." Abby Sutton sank deeper in the tub of mud beside Sloane's. Both of them had their hair wrapped in microfiber turbans.

"Well, don't." Sloane sighed, luxuriating in the warm mud as it melted the tension from her shoulders. "This was an unexpected surprise."

"I hope Benji unexpectedly surprises you again soon." Her mother took a sip of her smoothie.

Sloane's phone, sitting beside the mud bath, vibrated. She reluctantly pulled her hands from the mud, wiped them off and picked up the phone. There was a knot in her gut as she stared at the caller ID.

"Who is it?" her mother asked, noting her alarm.

"It's Delia."

"I thought Benji's family wasn't talking to you, and he wasn't talking to them."

That's why she was so surprised to see Delia's call. She didn't tell her mother that she'd been sending communications to Delia for months now, though Delia had yet to respond. The call rolled over to voice mail before she could answer, and Sloane was relieved. But it immediately started to ring again. This time she answered. "Hello, Delia."

"Sloane." Delia seemed surprised to hear her voice. "I wasn't sure you'd want to talk to me. If you didn't, I wouldn't blame you. We've been terrible to you."

Stunned, Sloane didn't respond.

"I'm sorry," Delia said. "I should've led with that. Sorry for all of the awful things I accused you of. I know you too well to think you'd ever knowingly hurt my brother."

"But?" There was hesitance in Delia's voice.

"But I'm not completely over it. I'm hurt that you kept this from me, that you were going to keep it from him. To be honest, that's what hurts the most. That you even considered doing that to Benji." Delia's voice wavered. "He loves those babies so much, and you were going to deprive them of their father."

"I know. He's such an amazing dad." Tears slid down Sloane's cheek and she sniffled. "I often think of what their lives would've been like if he hadn't come to Nashville that day. I would've ruined their lives and his, and I don't know if I can ever forgive myself for that, either."

"I believe you, and though you were completely wrong to keep this from him, I believe you thought you were doing the right thing." Delia sniffled again. "I'm not ready to make up today, but I wanted you to know that I'm trying because I miss my best friend."

"Me, too." Sloane couldn't stop the tears from falling.

"One more thing," Delia said. "This isn't an official Bennett apology. I'm only speaking for myself. My mother... Let's just say that she's not ready to make nice."

Sloane closed her eyes, more tears sliding down her cheeks when her friend disconnected the call.

It was the first step to repairing the friendship

that had been a lifeline for most of her life. Not having Delia in her corner for the past year had hurt.

"I know this is painful, honey, but it's progress." Her mother's voice was reassuring. Sloane wished her mother could hug her right now.

The phone rang again.

"Delia again?" her mother asked.

Sloane checked the caller ID. "No, it's Garrett Hyatt."

"Your old boss from the indie record company in Nashville? What does he want?"

Sloane had no clue. She answered the phone, trying to avoid getting mud on it.

"This is Sloane Sutton."

"Hey, Sloane. This is Garrett. It's been a while since—"

"You fired me?"

"You resigned," he said quickly, not mentioning the part where the company had asked her to resign. "Anyway, I just wanted to catch up and see how things have been going. I saw the pictures of the twins that you sent Natalie. Beau and Bailey are adorable kids. What are they now... about twelve months?"

"They're nine months, and thank you." Sloane inquired briefly about his wife and children and the rest of the team.

Abby mouthed, *What does he want?* and Sloane shrugged in response.

Garrett was telling a story about the latest antics of the lead singer of one of the label's most profitable acts when she cut him off. "Garrett, I'd love to catch up some other time, but I'm literally up to my elbows in mud right now. Is there something in particular I can do for you?"

"Yes, you can come and get your job. The one you earned and we should've given you in the first place."

"The creative director position? What happened to the woman you hired away from the big label?"

"She had the talk down, but the walk, not so much. Maybe it would've worked if we'd had her old label's budget, but she couldn't adjust to how we do things here, and she wasn't amenable to learning."

"That's too bad." Sloane studied her mud-caked nails, but didn't acknowledge his invitation.

"So what do you think?"

"About?"

"C'mon, Sloane. Don't be that way." Garrett was a brilliant record executive, but a mediocre human being. "So, about my offer—"

"I'm not in Nashville anymore," she said coolly. "I moved back to Magnolia Lake. On account of not having a job."

He cleared his throat again. "Like I said, I'm sorry about that whole ugly business. But if you take the creative director position, you'd be making twenty percent more—"

"Nope."

"Twenty-five percent—"

"Uh-uh."

"Thirty per—"

"If you're not offering at least a fifty percent increase and a signing bonus, I can just get back to my spa mud bath."

"You're at a spa right now?"

"Are you offering, or am I hanging up now?"

"Okay, okay. Look, I have to level with you here. We've got two major artists we're trying to re-sign. They're with the same agent and they're insisting that without you, there's no deal. Things here have been kind of crazy for the past few months. So I really need your help."

"Is that a yes on the money or are we moving the negotiation number higher?" She wiggled her toes in the mud.

"Yes, fine. Now will you come back?"

"Let me think about it. I need to consult with my family. I'll get back to you in a few days. Bye, Garrett." She hung up the phone and slipped down in the mud again.

"You've learned a lot from that wonder boy of yours, haven't you?" her mother laughed. "Gotta say, he'd be pretty proud of the way you handled yourself."

All of the tension returned to Sloane's shoulders. She'd gotten the job she'd always wanted at the salary she wanted. And she'd already found the perfect day care for the twins before she'd been fired.

But she couldn't have the job she wanted in Nashville and the life she'd made in Magnolia Lake with Benji, too.

She'd have to choose.

Sixteen

When Benji pulled into the driveway at the cabin, Atticus Ames's weathered pickup was parked in the driveway. The old man frequently visited the twins, and Beau and Bailey had their beloved PawPaw wrapped around their tiny little pinkies. But Benji had been agitated since his conversations with Parker and Delia, and he was in no mood to be cordial.

Sloane's grandfather sat in the great room bouncing Beau on his knee. The infant's adorable laugh filled the space, and Benji couldn't help smiling, despite the anxiety in his chest.

"Mr. Ames." Benji shook the older man's hand.

"Been thinking…" The man cleared his throat,

his focus still on Beau as he continued to bounce him on his knee. "There's no need to be so formal. We're practically family."

Little Beau reached eagerly toward Benji, chanting, "Da, Da, Da."

"Hey, buddy." Benji ruffled his young son's soft, curly hair and lifted him over his head, garnering more chuckles from Beau before he kissed his chubby cheek.

He turned back to Mr. Ames, not acknowledging the remark. He'd known the man all his life and always called him Mr. Ames. They weren't close enough for him to call him Gramps, as Sloane did. And he certainly wasn't going to call him by his first name.

"Is there anything I can get for you, sir?" Benji asked, despite his eagerness to spend some time with his son and daughter.

The man stood up and stroked his gray beard. "Just a few answers."

"About?" Benji raised a brow as he dodged Beau's slobby little hand grabbing for his beard.

"What are your intentions toward my granddaughter?" The old man yanked his pants up by the belt loops, hiking them higher on his waist. "I've kept my peace because Sloane, and Abby, asked me to stay out of it, but it's been a year. I gotta wonder, if my granddaughter is good enough to play house with, why ain't she good enough for you to marry?"

Sloane obviously hadn't told her grandfather about his earlier proposal, though given how he'd proposed, he couldn't blame her. But if she hadn't told him, it wasn't Benji's place to tell him now.

"Mr. Ames—"

"You've been extremely generous to our family, and I appreciate everything you've done for us. You've proven yourself to be a good man and a good provider. And it's obvious you have feelings for my granddaughter. But I won't stand by while you use Sloane and then toss her aside."

Okay, now he was getting pissed.

"I'm not using Sloane, and I have no intention of tossing her aside. I've always valued her and recognized what an amazing woman she is."

The older man lowered his gaze, not missing the verbal throat punch Benji had delivered.

"I haven't always been the best grandfather, but

it wasn't because I didn't love her. I wanted the very best for her, but I went about it all wrong. I've apologized to Sloane for that."

The man sat down again, as if the weight of the confession was too heavy for him to bear.

Livvie came into the room with Bailey on her hip. Benji kissed his smiling daughter, then asked Livvie to take the twins to their room so he and Mr. Ames could talk.

Once the door of the nursery clicked shut, Benji sat beside the old man on the sofa. "Look, I shouldn't have said that. It wasn't my place, and I'm sorry."

"I'm no fool, son. I know who I am. Who I've been. That I failed both Sloane and Abby. But I'm grateful that I've been afforded the opportunity to make amends." His expression was filled with pain and regret. "The bypass surgery I had, it gave me a new perspective on life. And these incredible kids of yours, they've given me a chance to finally get things right."

"I'm thankful you and Abby have been there for us from the beginning without question." Benji thought about his own family. "And I'm glad the twins have had the opportunity to get to know you."

"There's no doubt you love those kids, and I believe you love my granddaughter, too."

"I do love her." His voice was strained and there was tension in his neck and shoulders.

"Sounds like there's a *but* rattling around in there somewhere, son." The old man indicated Benji's chest.

Benji released a deep sigh. "Sometimes I wonder if I'm the only one emotionally invested in this relationship."

"You don't think Sloane cares about you?" Atticus asked incredulously. "Why else do you think she's here?"

Benji looked at the man pointedly.

"You're a man of means who can give my granddaughter anything she wants," he acknowledged. "But Sloane has never been one to mince words. If she didn't want to be here, son, you'd know it. And if she didn't care about you, you'd damn sure know that, too."

"Even if it was in her best interest to make me believe she did?" Though he'd defended Sloane to his cousin, Benji hadn't been able to let go of Parker's accusation.

"You obviously don't know Sloane very well." The old man stood and headed toward the front door.

"I do know Sloane, and I care for her and the twins more than anything in the world." Benji stood, too. "I honestly couldn't imagine my life without them. But it's hard to ignore the circumstances and what people around town are saying."

"Humph." Atticus turned back to him, his expression disapproving. "I actually believed you were a strong enough man to not let the gossips get inside your head. Evidently, I was wrong. If you'd think—even for a minute—that Sloane is capable of that kind of underhanded trickery…" He dragged a hand through his thinning, gray hair. "Well, maybe it's better if the two of you do part ways. For Sloane's sake, I hope it's sooner rather than later. Before she gets in any deeper."

"Mr. Ames… Atticus." Benji caught up with him on the porch and placed a hand on the man's shoulder, halting him. "I really do love Sloane, and I want to be with her."

The older man turned around, his gaze searching Benji's. His tone and expression softened. "Then let me offer you a bit of unsolicited advice, son. Don't make the mistakes I did. Don't leave Sloane wondering if you really love her. And don't try to control her. She'll fight you every step of the way, and I guarantee you'll be the one to lose."

With that, he shoved a baseball cap onto his head, got in his truck and drove off.

As the old man drove away, his shrewd advice replayed in Benji's head, already spinning from the day's events. One thing became abundantly clear: he and Sloane needed to sort things out. And it couldn't wait until her return.

Sloane slipped on her hotel robe and hurried to the door. Someone was knocking like a lunatic and it was well after ten at night. It had to be an emergency.

She peered through the peephole and quickly opened the door. "Benji, what's going on? Are Beau and Bailey okay?"

"They're great. I fed them and put them to bed for the night before I left them with Livvie."

"Is my grandfather okay?"

"He's fine." Benji closed the door behind him and entered the suite. Taking Sloane's hand, he led her to the sofa.

Sloane's heart still slammed against her chest. Something had to be very wrong.

"So what is it that you had to come all the way out here to tell me in person? It must be pretty important."

Benji inhaled deeply, and for a moment she thought he might hyperventilate. Finally, his gaze locked with hers.

"Sloane… I…" He cleared his throat and tried again, taking her hand in both of his. "Sloane Sutton, I love you. You and the kids, you're everything to me, and I don't ever want to be without you. I know I gave you until the twins' first birthday to decide whether you wanted to stay, but I couldn't wait any longer to tell you how I feel."

His meek smile reminded her of the little boy she'd first met all those years ago.

"You look stunned." He frowned. Lines spanned his forehead.

"Benji, I love being with you and raising the twins together, but as much as I love the family we've made, I can't ignore the damage I've done to yours." She wiped away tears with her free hand, and shook her head. "You've tried to hide it, but the pain of being alienated from your sister and your parents… It's always there."

"Is the rift between me and my family what's holding you back?" He cupped her cheek. "Honey, you can't blame yourself for that. Besides, Delia and I talked today."

"I know, and I'm hopeful about our relationship, but your mom hasn't budged."

He dropped his hand from her face. "Delia showed me the blog, told me about the emails. Why would you risk telling her about the money and being in breach of our agreement?"

"Because I broke your family. Just like I broke mine." Sloane wiped her face with the back of her hand. "I seem to have a gift for that."

"What are you talking about?" Benji frowned.

"When my mother got pregnant with me, it damaged her relationship with Gramps, and destroyed my father's relationship with his parents. And I'm the reason you've been estranged from your family this past year. When I heard the pain in Delia's voice today…" Sloane shook her head.

"I can't live with being the one who destroyed the Bennetts. And as long as we're together—"

"You'd be willing to walk away to fix things with my family?" Benji's voice grew quiet. "I appreciate how much you care for me, but Sloane, I'm a grown man. I made the choice to be with you, just like my mother and sister made their choices."

"You feel that way now, but what happens in two years when you look at me and see the woman who tore your family apart? Will you still love me then? Or will you wake up one day and hate me, the way my father did?"

"Honey, I could never feel that way about you or the twins." He held her in his arms as tears slid down her face, wetting his shirt. "I love you. I always have."

"That wasn't love, Benji, it was a crush." She freed herself from his embrace and turned to face him. "Sometimes I worry that's still what this is."

"Sloane." He pulled her onto his lap. "I know you don't believe it, but I honestly have been in love with you since I was ten. Back then, I didn't really understand how I felt. I just knew you were one of the most important people in the world to me, and that you always would be. Our past year together has only confirmed what I've always believed. We belong together."

She stared into his warm brown eyes, her heart full. There was so much she wanted to say, but the words wouldn't leave her mouth.

"Thank God for Blake and Savannah's wedding, for the weekend we spent at the cabin, for the twins…" he continued, undeterred by her silence. "Otherwise, I wouldn't be sitting here, holding you and telling you the thing I've always wanted to say. That I love you, Sloane, and I want to be with you. No matter what."

"I love you, Benjamin Darnell Bennett." She smiled as she leaned in to kiss him.

He cradled her face as his tongue met hers, heat building between them. Sloane unbuttoned his shirt, gliding her hand along the strong muscles of his hard chest.

Benji broke their kiss. His apologetic gaze met hers. "There's something else we need to talk about. At the wedding, when you told Kayleigh Jemison that you had a plan to get out of debt—"

"She thought I was talking about you?" Sloane asked incredulously. She and Kayleigh weren't close, but they knew each other well enough for it to sting that she would believe that of her. "Is that why she's been acting so weird whenever I see her around town?"

"Probably, but please don't be angry with her. She only mentioned it because—"

"She was afraid I was taking advantage of you." Sloane narrowed her eyes at Benji. "Wait… Is that what you think, too? That getting knocked up by a billionaire was my debt relief plan?" She scrambled off his lap and scampered to her feet.

When he didn't respond and his eyes didn't meet hers, it felt like he'd stabbed her in the heart.

"Sloane." Benji grabbed her hand and pulled her back onto his lap when she turned to walk away. "No, I don't believe you could be so cold and calculating. But I wouldn't have believed you'd keep the twins a secret from me, either."

She lowered her gaze. "I know it was wrong, but I honestly thought I was protecting you."

"Like you did when you broke our agreement and revealed our financial arrangement to Delia?" His voice was tense.

"I didn't want her to find out from someone else, and I couldn't stand being the reason you two weren't talking."

"If you felt that adamant about it, you should've

talked to me so we could work through it together." He blew out a frustrated breath. "Look, I
love you, Sloane. But if you want me to trust you
implicitly, you need to start trusting me. We need
to be equal partners in this relationship. I don't
want the kind of relationship my parents have.
Where one person exerts all the control and the
other is just along for the ride."

He was accusing her of behaving like his
mother. Worse, she'd given him valid reason.

"Benji, I'm sorry." Sloane squeezed his hand.
"I didn't realize that's what I was doing. That's
not what I want for us, either. I convinced myself I was only doing it for you, but maybe part
of it was me trying to take back some control
of my life. I went from being my own person to
you suddenly calling all the shots. Maybe I was
a little resentful."

"And for that, I apologize." He wrapped his
arms around her and pulled her closer as he
leaned back against the sofa. "Guess I was over-
compensating, not wanting to be too passive like
my father. I was also trying too hard to show you
that I'm not that little boy you still feel the need
to protect."

"We've got issues." Sloane smiled, and they both laughed.

"I'll tell you what, let's make a promise here and now that we won't keep secrets from each other and when it comes to our lives together, we're a team. So no more nanny ambushes, unexpected chefs or surprise interior design. Deal?"

"Deal." She pressed a quick kiss to his lips and smiled. "And you're absolutely sure this is what you want?"

"Never been more sure about anything." The humor in Benji's expression was gone. What she saw in his eyes was a love deeper than any she'd ever known. A love she couldn't bear to be without.

The solution to her Garrett problem was suddenly very clear. Her life in Nashville had been good, but the life she, Benji and the twins were building together in Magnolia Lake was far better.

Sloane opened her mouth to tell Benji about the job offer, but he kissed her again. A kiss that built slowly, but ignited a flame that quickly consumed them both.

He made love to her, and when she fell asleep in his arms, she knew without a doubt that this was exactly where she belonged.

Seventeen

Benji had an early breakfast with Sloane and her mother at the resort before heading back to the cabin to check on the twins. After spending a few hours with Beau and Bailey, he drove over to his parents' house.

He climbed the stairs of the home he'd lived in as a kid. His mother had already prepared the flower boxes on the porch.

Snapdragons.

He smiled, thinking of the bouquet of flowers he'd brought to Sloane on Valentine's Day when he'd returned from Japan. The day he'd first learned of the twins and had felt them moving inside their mother. A day he'd never forget.

Benji took a deep breath and pressed his thumb to the doorbell.

His father came to the door. A slow smile spread across the man's face and his eyes shone in the sunlight.

"Benji." Rick Bennett grabbed him in a bear hug and patted his back. "Son, it's so good to see you."

"You, too, Dad."

His father had emailed him, sent text messages and made the occasional call. All of it behind his mother's back, which had only made him angrier with his father for not taking a stand...until now.

"Delia showed me pictures of Beau and Bailey. They're beautiful, son." His father's eyes were watery. "I can't wait to meet them."

"We'll see how things go, Dad." Benji shoved his hands in his pockets as he followed his father inside the house.

"No." Rick Bennett turned around and pressed a palm to Benji's chest, halting him. "This ends today. This has been complete madness, and I've indulged your mother far too long on this. Regardless of what happens between you two, I'm ready to make my peace with you and Sloane. I want to see my grandbabies. *Today.*"

"Okay, Dad. Relax." Benji placed his hands on his father's shoulders. His dad had always been laid-back. It was strange to see him so fired up. "Where's Mom?"

"In the sunroom, pretending she didn't hear the doorbell." His dad jerked a thumb over his shoulder and frowned. "Good luck."

Benji didn't need luck. He'd never been so determined about anything in his life.

As long as Benji and his mother maintained this stalemate, he and Sloane would agonize over it in their own ways. And from what Delia had told him, things were just as bad for his mother and father. So he wouldn't take no for an answer.

When Benji entered the sunroom, his mother didn't look up from her crocheting. He leaned against the wall by the door. "So you're sending Parker to do your dirty work these days?"

"Benji." She spared him a brief glance, ignoring his statement. "I see you came alone."

"Why would I bring my family where they're not welcome?" He folded his arms.

She grimaced, as if his words had caused her

physical pain. "Seems you and Sloane have created your own little family. One you prefer over ours."

"Only because you made me choose," he said without apology.

She sighed quietly, raising her eyes to meet his after a few moments of silence between them. "Sit down, please. This is still your home, you know."

"Doesn't feel like it anymore, Mom." Benji sat on the sofa across from her. "Because home, for me, is wherever Sloane and the kids are."

Tears welled in his mother's eyes.

"Sloane certainly has cast a spell on you, hasn't she?" She set her work in the basket and turned her full attention to him. "I know you've always had a little crush on her, but I never imagined it would turn into something like this."

"I think the term you're looking for is *love*. I love Sloane, I love our kids, and I love our life together. And I wouldn't give it up for anyone or anything in the world. They mean everything to me, Mom."

"Sounds like you're all quite happy, then."

"We are, except for one thing that keeps looming over us. Sloane loves me, Mom. And she can't bear thinking that she's the reason you and I aren't talking."

"Well, she is," she said matter-of-factly.

"No, she isn't. That was the choice that you made." Benji scrubbed a hand down his face. "Whether you like it or not, Sloane is the woman I choose to be with. She and the twins make me happier than I've ever been. There is only one person who seems determined to destroy that happiness, and that's you."

"I just don't want to see you being taken advantage of by a girl like that."

"By a girl like *what*, Mom? Why is it that you hate Sloane so much? What has she ever done to deserve your distrust?"

"She was a bad influence on Delia."

"Seriously? You think Sloane was the bad influence?" Benji laughed bitterly. "It's time you and Delia have a heart-to-heart talk. If anything, you should be thanking Sloane for keeping Delia from getting in a lot more trouble than she did."

"I don't believe it."

"Talk to Delia, then get back to me." He stood up and headed to the door. "One more thing,

Mom. The woman you believe is a gold digger… I asked her to marry me the day I learned about the twins, but she turned me down cold. And as recently as last night, she was prepared to walk away rather than come between you and me. *That's* love."

His mother seemed genuinely stunned by both revelations. "Benji, what about Beau and Bailey? I'd really like to meet them."

"Once you've apologized to Sloane, I'd love for you to meet the twins." He turned back to her, his jaw tense and the sound of his heartbeat filling his ears. "That hasn't changed."

"Benji." She grabbed his arm before he could turn to leave, tears sliding down her cheeks. "I let this feud between us get out of hand, and I'm sorry, but you're my baby and… You've always had such a big heart. I just didn't want to see anyone take advantage of you."

"I know you only want what's best for me, Mom." The tension in his jaw eased a little. "But you need to trust that I know what that is."

She nodded, dabbing tears away. "Do you think tomorrow morning would be convenient for Sloane and I to talk?"

Benji gave his mother a quick hug and sighed. "Yes, I think that can be arranged."

Sloane paced the floor in the great room. She'd given the twins their baths, fed and dressed them. Now Livvie was entertaining them in the nursery.

Benji had offered to cancel his conference call so he could be there to give Sloane moral support. She'd insisted that he didn't need to coddle her. She'd be just fine. But now she wasn't so sure.

The doorbell rang and Sloane took one last deep breath before she opened the door and smiled. "Hello, Mrs. Bennett. Come in. Have a seat, please."

It felt odd welcoming the woman into the cabin they'd once owned.

"The renovations Benji made really do make it look completely different now." The older woman glanced around the space. "Cole's crew does excellent work."

"They certainly do. They did a fantastic job renovating my..." Sloane paused, realizing that wasn't a topic she wanted to discuss with the woman who already thought she was only with Benji for his money.

"About a year ago, my sister inadvertently mentioned that Cole had sent a crew to renovate a condo in Nashville. I suspected it was for you." It seemed to pain the woman not to make further comment about it. "But that's not why I'm here."

Sloane offered Mrs. Bennett coffee, water or sweet tea, but she declined. They both had a seat on the sofa in the great room.

"Look, Sloane, I was wrong," Benji's mother began without preamble. "And I fear I've always been wrong about you and your mother. I was so sure that you were going to bring my girl down. But from what Delia tells me, you were my secret ally, reining her in as much as you could."

"Delia was like a sister to me. It was my job to look after her," Sloane said, once she got over the initial shock of the apology.

"And as Benji's mother, I was only trying to do the same when I feared that you were taking advantage of him." The woman looked weary.

"I would never do that to him or to anyone." Sloane sat taller, determined to keep her cool.

"Benji believes that's true, and I've promised to trust his instincts about you."

"Thank you, Mrs. Bennett. That means a lot."

"It appears that you and my grandchildren mean the world to him." She smiled faintly. "Benji's never stood up to me like that before. I truly do believe he's been in love with you since he was a little boy. Leave it to Benji to find his soul mate at the age of ten."

"He told you that?" Sloane laughed, even as tears welled in her eyes.

"He did. I've learned quite a bit in the past twenty-four hours, and I've gotten to see you in a whole new light. Perhaps, I have been too hard on you all these years. I can't promise I'll change overnight, Sloane. But I do promise to give you a fair chance."

"That's all I ask." Sloane wiped away her tears. "By the way, I've spoken to Benji, and I'd really like to do a paternity test on the twins to put to rest any lingering doubts you may have."

"I appreciate the offer, Sloane," she said with a tight smile. "But I've seen pictures of Beau. He's the spitting image of his father. So please, don't go to any extraordinary lengths on my account."

Sloane nodded, her heart beating rapidly. She felt fiercely protective of her babies and a little nervous about Connie Bennett finally meeting them. Sloane stood, wringing her hands. "Would you like to meet the twins?"

Fat tears welled in the woman's eyes, too, as she nodded. "I'd like that very much."

Sloane went to the nursery and she and Livvie returned with her sweet babies. "Constance Bennett, I'd like you to meet your grandson and granddaughter, Beaumont and Bailey Bennett."

Benji's mother took them both in her arms and hugged them, her face wet with tears.

Eighteen

It had been more than a week since Benji's mother and father had met the twins. Two days ago, his sister and Evie had come to visit them, too. His niece had been enamored with her younger cousins and he'd never seen his sister or Sloane cry so many happy tears.

Benji checked his watch. He'd sent Sloane on an errand to Gatlinburg to give him time to finalize a few arrangements. Now, he'd been pacing the floor for more than twenty minutes and he'd already changed his shirt twice.

Everything had to be perfect.

He'd gone over the words he wanted to say to Sloane and the order in which he should say them. Debated whether he should start with his big ask or by telling her his big news.

He checked on the twins again, corralled in a large, colorful playpen so they couldn't get into anything.

Finally he heard the tires of her SUV crunch along the gravel up their drive and then the door slammed.

"Hey, babe. How was your trip into town?" He helped her bring in a few items.

"Great." She kissed him. "Did the twins give you any trouble?" She picked up each of them and kissed their little cheeks before returning them to the playpen. Then she went to the kitchen to start putting things away and he followed.

"Everything okay?" She narrowed her gaze at him. "You're acting a little weird."

Take it easy and relax.

"Everything is fine." He took her hand and led her to the couch. "I just need to tell you about an offer I got."

"Okay." She looked a little nervous.

He took a deep breath. "The company that bought mine, they want me to come back to Japan to help them work on a new project."

"Another six-month-long contract?"

"This time it'll be a year, and the money they're offering me to do this is insane."

"Wow, that's great." Her voice and expression indicated the exact opposite. "An entire year. Wow."

Opening and closing with a wow... Not good.

"Remember when I asked you to go to Japan with me and you listed all the things we could do together there? Well, here's our chance. And Beau and Bailey will get to travel the world before they're even two years old."

"That's a really incredible opportunity." She walked over to the fireplace, her back to him.

"Then why do you seem so miserable about it?" He followed her, wrapping his arms around her waist from behind. "Do you regret turning down the offer at the record company?"

"I don't regret choosing you, Beau and Bailey over fifty-hour work weeks. But maybe there is a little part of me that wishes I'd gotten to spend a little time doing the job. They came crawling to me, and I negotiated a fair salary. You would've been proud," she added faintly.

"I am proud of you, honey. You worked hard

for that creative director position and they offered it to you. So yes, I'm damn proud of you. And if you've reconsidered the offer, I'll support you one hundred percent."

"There's no way we can be together if I'm in Nashville and you're in Tokyo." She sank onto the sofa, glaring at him as if he'd gone insane.

"Don't worry, babe. We'll work it out." He sat beside her and traced her cheekbone with his thumb. "Trust me."

"That sounds awesome. Except for the part where it's completely impossible. Either you win, or I do. There's no way we both get what we want."

"Then it's simple. We move to Nashville. You take your dream job, and I'll become your incredibly rich househusband."

Sloane punched his arm playfully and laughed, laying her head on his chest. He draped an arm over her shoulder and pulled her against him.

"Don't be ridiculous. Your offer is probably worth more than I'd earn in a hundred years."

She wasn't wrong, but that didn't mean what she wanted wasn't important. He didn't need to work another day or do another deal ever. They'd still be fine and so would the kids.

"I've already achieved my holy grail."

"Building a company from scratch and selling it for two-point-five billion is a pretty hard act to follow."

"Not talking about that." He grinned. "I meant finally being with you. That's all I've ever wanted. So as long as I have you, Beau and Bailey, nothing else matters. I want you to go out in the world and do whatever it is that will make you as happy as you've made me."

"C'mon, Benj. Be serious."

"I am." He got on one knee and pulled out the diamond ring he'd been waiting to give her.

"Oh, my God." She pressed trembling fingers to her mouth. "It's beautiful, Benji. I love it."

"And I love you, Sloane. I've loved you most of my life. But what I feel for you now isn't a silly crush or lust or obligation or any of the things you were so worried this was. I genuinely love you. And I'm so lucky to have you in my life."

"I love you, too." She kissed him. "Just promise me that all of our crazy family issues won't become our issues."

"That I can promise you." He kissed her hand. "Say you'll marry me, Sloane. And we can live anywhere you want. Do whatever you want. As long as we're together."

She nodded eagerly, tears sliding down her cheeks. "Yes, yes, absolutely yes. I love you so much, Benji."

He slipped the ring on her finger and kissed her. Then he stood, pulling her into his arms.

"I can't believe we're finally gonna do this." She smiled, admiring the beautiful platinum-and-diamond solitaire ring flanked with smaller diamonds.

"Which reminds me." He pulled out his phone, sent a group text message, then returned it to his pocket.

Suddenly Sloane gripped his arm and pointed.

"What is it?" He looked where she was pointing. Bailey stood in the middle of the playpen, teetering on unsure legs.

"That's great, babe. But we've seen her do that lots of times."

"Shh…" She slipped her hand in his. "Wait for it."

Arms spread, Bailey looked up at them and

smiled. She took three steps toward them before falling onto her bottom again.

"I just saw my baby girl's first steps." He picked up the infant and kissed her plump cheek. She drooled on him and giggled.

Sloane picked up Beau, not wanting to leave him out. "Don't worry, sweetie. You'll be chasing your sister around the playpen in no time." She kissed his cheek, too.

Suddenly her eyes lit up.

"What is it?" Benji asked.

"I know where I want to live."

"Nashville or Tokyo?"

"Neither." She grinned. "I want us to build a house right here in Magnolia Lake, where the twins can grow up surrounded by our friends and family."

"So we pass on both opportunities?" He put Bailey, who was eager to try out her newfound skills, back down in the playpen.

Sloane put Beau down, too.

"It'll take at least six months for Cole to build our house here, right? It'd be nice to get some decent sushi and see the cherry blossoms while we're waiting."

"Are you sure about this, Sloane?"

She nodded. "Positive."

"You, soon-to-be Mrs. Bennett, are a genius." He hauled her against him, wondering if they had enough time to put the kids in their cribs and sneak off to their bedroom for a private celebration.

The front doorbell rang. *Apparently not.*

Marcellus carried in insulated food warmers and Benji went out to help him. Before they were done, his sister, niece and parents arrived. Then Abby and Atticus arrived in their truck, followed by Blake, Savannah and Davis. Zora, Parker, Max, Cole, and his uncle Duke and aunt Iris arrived soon after. Livvie and Mr. and Mrs. H filled out the rest of the party.

Benji watched as his parents fussed over the twins and Sloane showed off her ring.

They'd be very happy indeed living in Magnolia Lake.

* * * * *